BOOK REVIEWS

"A fun tale of adventure and mystery and romance. I loved it. An unique and lovely story of friends and love and danger and accepting yourself. Everything about this book was simply wonderful. I look forward to reading more from this author." Michaela ~ BookBub Reviewer

"Melody Archer's characters Rory and Gabe have known each other since she was six and came to live with her three Aunts of Great Grandfather's island. She has loved him since she was 16, now it is time to win his love with a Fake Marriage. But someone wants Rory dead by her 21st Birthday. Wonderful characters, funny, caring and loving. Highly recommend!" Patty ~ Amazon Reviewer

THE BILLIONAIRE'S MARRIAGE PROMISE

MELODY ARCHER

WANT MORE SWEET ROMANCE?

Eliza and Daniel Stevenson's Love Story is *waiting for you to enjoy!* Simply, click the link below to grab your copy of this FREE Sweet Romance :) Go here: https://www.melodyarcher.com/free-book/

"Thou sword of truth, fly swift and sure, that evil die and good endure…" Flora *from Sleeping Beauty*

CHAPTER ONE

abe

"YOU HAVE millions of loyal followers worldwide. It's plain to see you've helped a lot of people turn their lives around with your online mentoring programs, books and events."

Winny O, the most popular International Daytime Talk Show host sat across from Gabe Stevenson as loud cheers from the studio audience echoed off the walls.

Gabe smiled and shifted slightly, uncomfortable with the praise. He nodded towards the audience before turning his blue-eyed gaze back to his host.

Her unwavering gaze swept over him.

Returning a casual smile, he tried to hide his shaky

hands. He gently squeezed the paper clip hidden in the palm of his hand. It was his usual reminder to focus so nervous jitters didn't get the better of him.

"I feel like most of what we know about you is from your programs. But most of us don't know the real Gabe Stevenson. Why don't you take a few minutes to share your story?" Winny O's brown eyes held a challenge that was familiar to the millions of viewers who watched her weekly show.

"That's a tall order but I'll do my best." Gabe leaned back on the soft studio chair and adjusted the sleeves of his blue designer sweater.

This was always the toughest part of any interview.

"I was born and raised in Paradise Lake, a small town not too far from Seattle. I was the middle child of five sons born to the best parents we could ask for. My brothers and I had a great childhood spending time doing activities and having fun with each other and with our mom and dad. But, all that ended suddenly one day when my Dad died of a heart attack. I was thirteen years old." Emotion clogged his throat and he swallowed convulsively as memories invaded his senses.

He stared down at his feet for a moment and rubbed the back of his neck willing himself to regain control of churning emotions.

Taking a deep breath he looked up again blinking back tears as he thought of his Dad. "His death was sudden and unexpected. The doctor said it was caused by stress. We learned that his business partner had taken all the money out of their shared accounts and he'd found a way to access my Dad's personal account as well. We were wiped out. It was a really difficult time for all of us."

"I bet it was." Winny O's brows puckered in concern and she looked at her audience before returning her gaze to him. "Did you go through a period of time wondering what happened?"

Gabe shifted uncomfortably in his chair. "Yes. I had many questions for years."

"Would you share a few of them?"

"Sure. Even though I was thirteen years old, I went through self-blame and wondered what I could have done differently to help my Dad not be so vulnerable to sabotage. I also remembered feeling back then that there was something I didn't like about my Dad's business partner."

He paused before he spoke again. "At the time I should've paid more attention, acted on those misgivings and did more investigating. Maybe I could've prevented the stress my Dad suffered and maybe he wouldn't have had a heart attack." His voice cracked and Gabe swallowed back the emotion that clogged his throat. Even though he tried to stop it a stray tear escaped one eye anyway.

Winny O silently handed him a box of tissues, waiting for a few moments before she asked, "Did any of your questions or fears from what you saw your Dad go through contribute to the reasons you began your self-development training?"

"Absolutely. I wanted to do whatever I could to help other people so they would be better prepared for life and to overcome any trouble they would face."

"I can understand that." She nodded. "Please continue."

Gabe looked out at the studio audience before turning

back to Winny. "After the police did their investigation, my Dad's partner was convicted of his crimes and went to jail. But, that didn't change the fact that my father was still gone from our lives. We were left scrambling trying to put the pieces back together of our shattered family."

He hesitated as compassionate sighs erupted from the studio audience. "It was especially hard for my mom to make ends meet, so me and my four brothers helped out. My two older brothers, Adam and Jack started working full-time and I found part-time work after school. I was thirteen at the time."

"What work did you find at such a young age?"

"I started hauling newspapers after school for a couple years. By the time I reached High School I was working for a local TV station as a student reporter. They wanted to get a bird's eye view of an average student's thoughts on different issues that affected the town."

Winny O eyes twinkled. "Sounds like the perfect job for you."

"It really was. The only drawback was when a couple of friends at the time tried to use my new job as a reporter to get on TV. My girlfriend tried that when she asked me to interview members of her book club."

"I showed up and she was the only person there. It turned out it wasn't really an interview for the book club she wanted. She admitted to being jealous of my growing popularity in High School and that she wanted to be on television. She wanted to be famous."

"Needless to say our relationship didn't last. I couldn't be in a relationship with someone I couldn't trust." Gabe grimaced and looked at the audience.

His host shook her head from side to side her brows puckered as she looked at the studio audience. Returning her gaze to Gabe, Winny signalled for the cameraman to zoom in and get a closer shot.

"It's seems like you've experienced a few times in your life when people you trusted maneuvered their way into your life in a way that made it difficult."

Gabe nodded. "I guess that's true. I wish I would've known back then what I know now."

"Most of us I'm sure would agree that hindsight helps us see things clearer." Winny looked out at her audience and sighed. "But let's switch to something more recent. Not long ago, I read in Seattle's business magazine that your date to the Benefit Gala told a reporter that you were getting married. Is there any truth to that?"

"Sadly, no. We hadn't got to the point in our relationship where we had talked about marriage. Needless to say, we are no longer together." Gabe expelled a breath as he remembered how Maddie had burst into his interview with a reporter at the Benefit Gala and casually hinted they would be married soon.

It really frustrated him when people thought he could be so easily managed.

"Were those experiences the inspiration behind starting your career?" His host cocked her head slightly to the side, her gaze intense.

Gabe sighed. "For the most part, yes. After my dad died I was devastated. I'd just lost my best friend and mentor and the man who encouraged me everyday. Along with that, a deeper awareness that my Dad's friend had betrayed him really hit home and was difficult for me to process." Gabe shifted uncomfortably.

"I wanted to grow up to be like the man I most admired, my Dad. But, I also wanted to learn how to do whatever it took to prevent people from sabotaging my family. That led me to spending time at our local Library whenever I could to read all about how to become a better person and develop a success mindset. I started learning as a teenager and I continued to learn until finally in college I began writing about personal development on a blog and talking on the subject on podcasts and videos."

"According to comments from thousands of people around the world, you've certainly helped many people and given them hope. I think that speaks for itself."

"Thanks so much, Winny. That means a lot coming from you." Gabe smiled as he reflected. "What I really want to do is to help as many people as possible learn how they can live each day with joy, to love themselves better and to help them reach out to others to make their dent in the world."

Loud clapping from the studio audience filled the room.

Gabe nodded and smiled warmly. Their show of appreciation for his work meant a lot to him.

"I see your family is here. From their happy smiles, I can see they're proud of you."

He looked at his mom, his brothers and their wives and his grandparents who were seated in the front row.

They nodded as the camera panned towards them. Gabe saw his mom was a little misty-eyed, while the faces of his other family members held big grins.

Gratefulness for his family welled up inside him. "Everyday I'm thankful for their love and support."

"Support from family is so important." Gabe turned to see them nod vigorously. Winny O shifted back to him and the camera zoomed in for a close-up. "Looks like you have everything. Perhaps with the exception of the one thing most men want."

Bracing himself at Winny's comment something compelled him to ask. "What's that?"

"A woman to love." His host paused and Gabe squirmed a little, becoming really uncomfortable with where these questions were going. "Tell us, have you ever had a serious relationship or been married?"

Brown eyes challenged his and he couldn't look away. Gabe could feel prickly heat rising up to his cheeks. He should've known his host would dig deeper and ask the one question he'd been able to avoid in most interviews.

He responded quickly. "No I haven't. It's never been a priority."

"Hmm." She looked him over as if doubting the truth of his words. "Is it true that your marital status might be changing soon?"

Gabe's neck and cheeks felt like they were on fire.

He looked over at the crowd who seemed to be waiting for his answer with baited breath. Turning back to Winny O he decided to play dumb. "What do you mean?"

"Well, I read last month's article in one of Seattle's most popular magazines questioning whether you'd be single for long. I'm sure there are many single women out there wondering the same thing." Winny grinned.

"So I wanted to ask, are the rumors true that your

great-grandfather Walker Stevenson setup his will in a way that required all five of his great-grandsons to marry by their twenty-seventh birthday to receive their inheritance?"

Gabe uttered a low groan. He should've realized that at least one reporter would have found out the details of Grand's will. It seemed like he was doomed to answer the one question he hoped to avoid. "Yes absurd as it sounds, it's true."

"How long do you have until the deadline?"

"A little over six weeks." Gabe had given himself more time to look for a wife than his older brothers had done. He liked to plan things out ahead of time. Yet even though he'd been looking for a woman to marry for almost a year now no one had appealed to him. Now all he had was six weeks left to find a wife.

"So not a whole lot of time to find the woman you want to marry."

Gabe grimaced and nodded as heat crawl up his neck. He really didn't like where this conversation was going.

"If you don't mind my asking, what do you inherit if you decide to go along with his wishes?"

It looked like Winny O was focused on the topic of his upcoming marriage and he was stuck answering her questions. "Well, Grand decided to give me his Island. Most folks around Paradise Lake know the place as Walker's Island. It's about an hour away from Paradise Lake. The only buildings on the land are Grand's hunting lodge, a small guest house and a small cottage."

Gabe winced inwardly at the sighs coming from the crowd. He really didn't want to talk about Grand's ridiculous will requirement, but it looked like that Pandora's box was now wide open.

"Sounds like a great place to get away from the bustle of everyday life."

"Yeah it's great. I have great memories of fishing and sailing every summer with my Dad, Granddad and Grand when I was a kid." A warmth of belonging filled Gabe as he remembered the pleasure of being with his Dad enjoying being on the water surrounding Walker's Island.

Winny smiled broadly. "With so many great memories attached to Walker's Island have you thought about going along with your great-grandfather's last wishes?"

He turned toward the audience and cringed at the wide-eyed gazes that stared back at him. Suddenly Gabe wished he could disappear.

Why had Winny chosen to focus her interest on whether or not he was getting married? He squeezed the paperclip in his hand once more reminding himself to play it cool and smile.

"I'm thinking about it."

"What's stopping you from saying yes?"

"I've never found a woman I love and with whom I want to spend the rest of my life. I'm starting to doubt she's out there."

She leaned a little closer. "Maybe some of those fears you mentioned earlier are holding you back. Maybe you'll discover when you let go of your fear of being vulnerable, you'll find yourself falling in love with the woman you want to marry."

A knot coiled in his stomach at her words. He didn't want to admit that any of her words were true.

It wasn't fair his host was shining a magnifying glass on all his weaknesses. But he remembered this was exactly what made people choose Winny O's Daytime TV show over many others.

She was very good at getting down to the heart of things.

Yet he still doubted there was a woman out there who wouldn't try to manipulate him. He doubted there was a woman who wouldn't demand more than he had to give.

Before Gabe could comment she continued, "Are you telling me you have never fallen in love?"

Heat prickled his skin sending another wave of irritating discomfort down his body. Maybe it was time he answered Winny's questions a little differently. Maybe just this once he could veer her off track. "Not recently. But years ago there was one girl that I loved and asked to marry me."

"Oh, do tell."

Gabe enjoyed the moment filled with gasps and wide-eyed surprise. "This girl was beautiful with long blond hair. She lived by the beach and was always out searching in the water for another rock or plant. I taught her how to sail on my sailboat and she taught me how to find wonderful plants and creatures under the water. We became good friends."

"Go on. You said you asked her to marry you."

He nodded. "She was scared of being alone. Her parents had died and all she had were three Aunts who were getting on in age. I told her I would marry her and then she wouldn't need to be alone or scared." Gabe grinned as he heard *oos* and *ahs* coming from the studio audience.

"Did she agree?"

"She told me it would be hard to wait, but she'd marry me."

Winny raised an eyebrow, waiting.

Gabe reminded himself that honesty needed to prevail. "I should fess up and tell you this girl was six years old at the time."

Winny O sent him a I-can't-believe-you-just did-that grimace. He could hear his brothers' chuckle from the front row, but no one else seemed to appreciate his sense of humor.

For a fleeting moment, Gabe thought of the scared little girl who had captured his heart all those years ago. He wondered how Rory was doing now. It had been years since he'd last seen her.

"Well, maybe that's where you should start in your search for a bride Gabe." His host leaned back on her chair and winked, before turning to her audience. Soon they began to chant 'yes' and Winny O looked at him with a big grin. "Go find this girl. See if she will agree to marry you now that she's all grown up."

The corners of his lips turned up slowly. "Maybe I will."

His host nodded. "Thanks Gabe for joining us here on the Winny O Show."

"Thanks for your kind invitation. It was my pleasure."

She looked directly into the camera. "There you have it folks. That was Gabe Stevenson, also known as the number one personal development mentor in the nation.

Keep an eye on Gabe in the months to come. He might surprise us yet and suddenly find and marry the woman he loves."

Gabe Stevenson managed to keep his hundred watt white smile that attracted thousands, intact. His Grandmom had coined the phrase to describe his wide grin and right now he hoped it would deliver.

He couldn't wait to be with his family again. He needed time to simply be himself away from the crowds.

❧

"THAT WAS a great interview last week Gabe." His brother Jack came to stand beside him at the helm of his yacht.

Gabe grinned as he steered his yacht *Lady Eliza*, along Puget Sound waterway. "Yeah. But I must admit many of Winny O's questions were unexpected and somewhat unnerving."

"Like when she started asking about the requirements of Grand's inheritance or if you'd ever been in love?"

"Exactly." Gabe shook his head in silence for a moment remembering how uncomfortable he'd been sharing his personal life with Winny O's international audience.

"That's understandable." Jack spoke as he looked across the wide waterway before turning his gaze back at Gabe.

Gabe peered over at his brother and grimaced at the calculated look in his eyes. "What?"

Jack stood there for a moment longer before he spoke. "Just wondering if you've decided to agree to Grand's terms so you can get your inheritance?"

Steering the yacht forward Gabe sighed as he saw

Walker's Island in the distance. A wave of longing rose up on the inside to own the one piece of land that had given him a sense of belonging and been a huge part of his childhood. Was the price of marriage worth it?

"To my way of thinking Grand made the price a little too high for his great-grandsons to receive their inheritance." Gabe expelled a breath frustrated that marriage was being forced on him.

"Yeah, I understand how you feel." Jack's half smile played around the corners of his mouth. "I was annoyed too when I first realized in order to get my hands on that silver mine I would need to marry."

"What made you decide it was worth the price?"

"I was desperate to own the mine and to discover the treasures inside it. Grand convinced me those treasures were there when I was just a boy. Turns out he was right."

Gabe nodded thinking of how only a few months ago Jack and his team of miners had discovered a deep vein of silver and a few days later they found a small vein of gold.

"But the biggest treasure was marrying Bella." Jack smiled the same sappy smile he'd had on his face since he married his wife a year ago.

"Well not all of us can be lucky enough to have a marriage that turns out as well as yours." Gabe was happy for his older brother but at the same time the fact that he had to marry made him feel trapped.

If he were honest, it was fear of getting too close and letting himself be vulnerable to a woman again that had him real worried.

"We definitely didn't begin by thinking our marriage would work. If you remember Bella and I agreed to a marriage-of-convenience right from the start. The only reason we agreed was because we both benefited."

"Our marriage certainly hasn't been without it's difficult moments, but we fell in love and we are very blessed to have each other. Who's to say you won't find a woman who'll be the right person for you too?" Jack persisted in his usual way trying to dig out problems and fix them.

"I just don't know Jack. I've become very wary of women, based on my experiences in the past. Especially those who have tried to get close to me in order to get what they want." Gabe did his best to dispel the terrible memories.

"I understand. I have vivid reminders of what that's like from my first marriage." Jack hesitated. His brother's brow puckered and Gabe could only imagine the unpleasant memories that surfaced.

He remembered Elin and the abrupt way she'd rejected Jack after he arrived home with a scar. She hadn't even cared about the fact that her husband had received the scar because he had heroically saved a teenager from being kidnapped by a human trafficking gang. Only a short time later, Jack's wife and unborn son had died suddenly in a car accident.

"I know you do man. Sorry you had to go through all that." Gabe was amazed that even though his brother went through so many difficulties he kept his fighting spirit.

Jack hesitated for a moment before he spoke again. "But regardless of my own doubts I found someone to marry who is amazing and whom I love with all my heart. I think you owe it to yourself to see if there is someone out there for you. Grand believed that finding a wife was a good thing. He wanted that for each of his great-grand-sons. I've come to believe he was on to something."

Jack bumped Gabe's shoulder with a familiar cama-raderie he remembered from when they were kids.

Gabe released a deep sigh realizing it was time for him to make a decision. "Maybe you're right. Like you and Adam, maybe I'll find a woman who will agree to a marriage-of-convenience. I might take a page from your book and see what happens."

"Now you're talkin'." Jack clapped him on the back. "You never know Gabe. Maybe love is waiting for you just around the corner."

"I don't know about that. But, we'll see what happens." Gabe still had serious doubts that there was an unattached female anywhere whom he would trust enough to marry.

However, he was willing to agree to a marriage-of-convenience. That way if they had no emotional ties after one year they could part ways with no hard feelings.

Gabe was suddenly pulled out of his reverie by childish belly laughter behind them. Jack hurried back to the salon where his nine-month old son Walker was playing with his cousin Daniel.

Seeing his Mom sitting on the floor of the salon and his family gathered nearby stirred a warmth inside him. His brothers' wives Elle and Bella were enjoying a cup of tea, laughing and talking together.

His younger brothers Luke and Zach were playing chess. Granddad dozed while Grandmom was busy crocheting another set of baby socks.

He couldn't deny the longing that rose up inside him to have a family someday.

Gabe looked at the horizon and saw Walker's Island getting closer. He had convinced his brothers and their wives, his grandparents and his Mom to join him to visit the Island and take a look at Grand's old Hunting Lodge.

He needed to take a look at the place and see what needed to be fixed up. His plan was to live there again for a little while as he took a break from his fast paced schedule.

Focusing, he steered his large Yacht closer to Walker's Island.

As the pier drew near, Gabe slowed the engine until he could swing up next to the dock. He was thankful years ago Grand had built a long sturdy pier so large boats could set down anchor near the island.

After they stopped he walked with his family down the dock toward the sandy beach.

He could see the chimney top of Grand's Hunting Lodge straight ahead, partially hidden behind rows of tall trees that circled Walker's Island.

Without warning, loud barks shattered the silence followed by splashing sounds.

Gabe turned for a quick look at the beach. He saw two dogs running along the water's edge chasing each other. A young woman stood in the water with her hands on her hips. Her long blond ponytail flowed in the wind and her bubbling laughter caught his attention.

For a moment he stood mesmerized, staring at the beautiful woman standing in front of him.

Rory Shepard.

Memories flooded him of the last time he'd seen her.

She'd been sixteen and he'd been on the Island enjoying two weeks that summer with Grand.

At the time he'd been so busy with college and starting his business that he hadn't taken the time to really appreciate those around him. Gabe regretted it later as that had been the last summer he enjoyed time on the Island with Grand before he passed away.

They had a picnic on the beach with Grand, Rory and her three aunts. Later on they all went sailing.

Gabe taught Rory how to sail and he'd been able to get closer to her. She was beautiful even back then. But she was naive and too trusting of others, including him.

He'd been attracted to her that last summer. For that reason he'd sent her a note that he couldn't make it to their last time sailing together.

He had left the Island suddenly the next day with Grand.

Regret coiled like a snake in his belly at how shabbily he'd treated her.

He couldn't admit his attraction to her so he left.

Looking back, Gabe saw his sudden departure as the cowards way out that it was.

Rory had always been like a little sister.

They weren't related, but all those summers on the Island when he'd taught her snorkeling, fishing and sailing made him feel like an older brother.

The summer Rory had turned sixteen had been a turning point.

The sudden realization hit him hard, like a wave breaching the protective walls of a fortress. His childhood friend had blossomed into a beautiful woman.

He'd felt himself drawn to her in a way he'd never felt before or since.

That new attraction had scared him. He'd left Walker's Island for fear that if he stayed, he would give into his desires.

Back then he thought more about how he could protect himself rather than what others needed.

Rory had always been someone who thought of others before herself.

Her selfless giving was what had always captivated him along with her beautiful face and form.

That summer she'd told him that someday she wanted a family of her own to love. He couldn't believe how naive she was about love. Or was it that he was cynical?

The corners of his lips turned up as he remembered.

Without conscious thought Gabe walked towards her.

Rory stood in a small inlet of water surrounded by trees. She pulled green plants from under the water and tossed them into a bucket at her side.

Gabe walked until he stood behind her. He had to admit he enjoyed the view. He grinned. "You still love searching for plants and sea creatures I see."

Rory looked up startled and fell backwards into the water.

He hurried over and reached out a hand to help her up.

Guilt flooded his senses for shocking her and causing her to fall in the water.

Large violet eyes widened even further and she stared at him, unmoving.

Hesitantly, she reached up with one hand and with her other clutched long green seaweeds. As Gabe pulled her out of the water he tugged a little too hard and Rory fell against his chest.

"Sorry." Gabe held her wet shivering body close to his. He looked down into the same beautiful violet blue eyes that he remembered from years ago.

"Gabe. You came back." Rory breathed out his name as she clung to him. Long dark eyelashes encircled violet eyes like sparkling diamonds in the morning sun.

Holding her close was doing crazy things to his heart. The urge to lower his head and touch his lips to hers was almost overpowering.

He expelled a breath as suddenly dogs barked loudly beside them. He released his grip on her.

Rory quickly stepped back and out of his arms.

The sudden sense of loss was so acute, Gabe clenched his hands into tight fists to stop himself from reaching for her once more.

"Latte and Mocha hush." She patted each of her dogs on the head when they obeyed her command.

Rory tossed the dripping seaweed into the bucket beside her and wiped her hands on the drying cloth tucked into the waistband of her shorts.

Peering up at him she whispered. "Are you back to stay?"

Rory's face clouded with a mixture hurt and fear.

Gabe resisted the urge to wrap his arms around her. He hesitated before replying. "For a few weeks anyway. Grand decided Walker's Island was to be part of my inheritance, so I thought I'd fix up the Hunting Lodge."

"Sorry to hear about your great grandfather's passing. I adored that man. He will be missed."

"Grand always thought well of you and your three aunts."

"I'm glad. We thought the world of him too." Rory's eyes turned a little misty as they talked about Grand and she looked away.

Warmth flooded him. He couldn't remember the last time a woman of his acquaintance had been moved to tears from the passing of someone she loved. Her simple and honest emotions were refreshing.

Rory crossed her arms over her chest a furrow forming between her brows. "Years ago you left the island without saying a proper goodbye. You still owe me a day sailing."

Heat crawled up his neck to his cheeks as he remembered. "Sorry about not saying goodbye, Rory. You have every right to be angry." He grimaced and looked out at the water for a moment, before turning to look back at her. "Can I take you sailing at the usual time on Friday?"

She ran a hand along her wet arms, taking a long time to answer him. "I suppose. I'm not so sure just one sailing trip will make up for it. But it's a start."

Gabe laughed realizing that he probably did owe her more than one day on his sailboat. "We'll plan for a few trips then how does that sound?"

"Much better." Rory shivered and rubbed her arms.

"You're freezing. Let me help." Gabe quickly pulled off his hoodie and slipped it around her shivering body. "If your aunts are home tomorrow, I was planning to stop by. Grand had something he wanted me to give them."

Rory smiled. "Oh, I've no doubt my three aunts will be happy to see you. Why don't you stop by for lunch?"

Lifting the pail of seaweed, she held it in front of her like a protective shield.

"I'll do that."

"Good." She pulled the hoodie tighter around herself before turning to look at him. "I must get home. My aunts will be wondering what kept me. See you tomorrow. " Rory quickly nodded and hurried away, dogs following her every step.

Gabe watched her slender figure as she hurried along the trail away from him.

His childhood friend was a child no longer. The woman she had become was even more beautiful than he remembered.

Yet, there was something else. Something had changed. It was like a cloud of fear hung over her.

Gabe didn't know what had happened in her life during the five years since he'd last seen Rory but he was determined to find out.

Walking back to Grand's Hunting Lodge, Gabe found himself looking forward to see her again. Vivid memories surfaced of the naive little girl from years ago pestering him with questions or showing him her latest discovery on the beach.

He shook his head from side to side. A voice in his head spoke up. *Gabe she's not that little girl anymore. Now Rory has become a beautiful woman. Admit it. You are still attracted to her.*

Gabe turned again to watch his childhood friend until she faded behind tall trees in the distance.

He was going to be in her company a lot over the next

couple weeks. There was no way he could let his attraction to Rory get out of control.

This time he would need to be vigilant.

This time he would need to do everything in his power to guard his heart.

This time he would need to keep his distance from the one woman who captivated him.

CHAPTER TWO

ory

HURRYING along the winding dirt trail back to the cottage Rory's thoughts were filled with Gabe.

She shivered, but this time it wasn't from the cold.

This time she trembled at the memory of being held in Gabe Stevenson's arms.

When he'd pulled her up out of the water and held her in his strong arms she'd all but melted. Her heart beat accelerated and warm tingles ran the length of her body at his touch.

Peering into his vivid blue eyes, she'd glimpsed his surprise and something more. Appreciation? His gaze lowered to her lips before he suddenly stopped himself and stepped away.

For years she had dreamed of Gabe's kisses, but they

had never crossed that line. Rory knew he looked on her more as a little sister than as a woman he could date.

Maybe it was better that way.

She didn't need the added worry of something happening to another person she loved.

Memories clouded her thoughts of the fire that had killed her parents. She ran a shaky hand through her wet hair. Recently her aunts had been targeted by someone threatening to harm them.

Rory feared somehow it was all her fault that people she loved were hurt or worse.

Hurrying up the steps to the backdoor of their cottage she ran into the kitchen.

"Rory there you are. We were all set to come looking for you." Her Aunt's slender form bustled back and forth between the stove and the mixer. She was a whirlwind who loved to be either in the kitchen cooking or outside gardening.

"Aunt Florrie, I was just getting more seaweed. It's a sunny day for it." Rory kissed her on the cheek and breathed deeply of the chicken and vegetable soup. "Dinner smells so good."

"It'll be finished soon. I'll turn the pot down to simmer so we can set the seaweed on the drying pans in the backyard."

"Thanks. I'll go find Aunt Merrie and see if she has time to help." Rory grabbed one of the sliced carrots and popped it into her mouth. She had just turned around to head up the stairs when her other Aunt walked into the room leaning heavily on her cane.

Aunt Fawn was the oldest of her three aunts. Just last

week they had celebrated Aunt Fawn's sixtieth birthday. This past year she'd suffered more health problems with her rheumatism flaring up at different times. Rory didn't like to ask her for help for fear it would make things worse.

Yet, because of Aunt Fawn's ailments she was constantly worried about everyone else's health. "Oh my dear you're all wet. You should go change your clothes. You don't want to catch your death."

Rory leaned close and kissed Aunt Fawn's soft cheek. "I'll do that. Be back soon."

She hurried up the stairs to her bedroom and slipped out of her wet clothes and into her practical work shirt and jeans.

Thoughts of Gabe continued to drift through her mind. No big surprise there. After all these years her childhood friend never left her thoughts for long.

Walking over to her writing desk she glanced at the index cards and notebooks filled with story ideas.

With gentle fingers she traced the row of romance books on her bookshelf that she'd written since she was fourteen. More evidence of Gabe's influence on her life. Her attraction to him had given her a way to express her longing for love through writing even though she couldn't have the man himself.

She sighed.

Now Gabe was back on the Island to stay for a few weeks. How would she be able to be near her childhood friend without revealing her attraction to him?

You'll simply need to guard your heart and not let Gabe get too close. You can do this. The voice in her head sounded very confident. Hopefully she would stick to her resolve and keep her distance from him.

Yet how could she keep her distance and at the same time ask for his help? She really needed his help to figure out who was behind all the strange incidents that had been happening on the Island.

Biting her lip she thought of her three aunts. She would do everything she could to protect them. But, they refused to leave Walker's Island because they loved it here. This was their home and they couldn't imagine living anywhere else.

After all they had moved here because of her. They had been trying to protect their sister's only daughter.

This beautiful Island had been the only home that was vivid in Rory's memory. Only vague memories flitted through her mind of the house she grew up in with her parents. They'd moved here right after her sixth birthday party — the same party that ended with a house fire and her parents tragic death.

She shuddered and fingered the heart-shaped locket her mom had given her on her sixth birthday.

Waves of sadness rolled over her.

Rory shook her head in a desperate attempt to dispel the horrible memories. She couldn't think of that right now.

It had been right after she had lost her parents that her three aunts had finally accepted Walker Stevenson's offer to live in this cottage on the Island. They had saved his life years ago and he told her Aunts he wanted to do something for them.

Gabe's great-grandfather had assured them they could

live rent-free for the rest of their lives in the cottage on Walker's Island.

When Rory was six years old they moved to this beautiful place.

Through the years Rory grew to love it here even though at times it was a little lonely. Twice a month they took the boat to the small town of Paradise Lake.

That's how she had the chance to make a few friends her age like Bella and Razelle. They had been such good friends. Rory had spent time with them and they had helped each other over the years.

Bella had helped her find a publisher for her first romance novel years ago and Raz had helped her research plants that would help create wonderful skincare creams to help with her aunts skin problems.

As it turned out both the novels and developing the skincare creams had been just what Rory needed to do.

She never imagined her novels would become popular. The money she earned from novels had helped her aunts to fix the house and she'd been able to get the equipment she needed to continue to develop the skin care products.

It was a start.

She said a prayer of thanks that she'd finally had a breakthrough as she experimented with mixtures of seaweed, botanicals, marine algae and essential oils. Her aunts skin care troubles were getting better.

Glancing at the boxes of bottles and labels that were stacked near her desk she shook herself out of her daydream.

The work wasn't going to get done by itself.

Quickly she opened her bedroom door and hurried down the hallway toward her Aunt's room.

"Aunt Merrie can I come in?" After several knocks she slowly opened the door knowing that sometimes her aunt got caught up in her work.

At the sound of the squeaky door, her aunt turned quickly placing her hand on her chest. "Oh my Rory. You startled me."

"Sorry Auntie. You busy?"

"I promised your Aunt Florrie I would type up her recipes and make a book out of them. But I'm struggling to read some of her writing." Aunt Merrie lifted a sheet of paper with scrawled writing toward the window. Pushing her glasses up her nose she squinted trying to see the words better.

Rory leaned closer to try to help her. "It is hard to read. Maybe we should ask Aunt Florrie."

"I think you're right. Florrie is a good cook but not so good at writing. I guess that's why we sisters need each other, right?"

Rory hugged her Aunt and opened the door. "Right. Hey, while you have a moment could you help us organize and clean the large piles seaweed?"

Aunt Merrie followed Rory down the stairs and spoke with a mischievous smile hovering over her lips. "Oh, this was just a ploy to get me downstairs so you could put me to work?"

"Not very subtle I suppose." Rory grinned.

"No. But I'm always happy to help you Rory." Aunt Merrie squeezed her in a tight hug.

Rory hugged her back and they hurried out the back door.

Together they had made the backyard larger adding a tall wooden fence around the perimeter to keep out the wild animals.

When Rory started High School Aunt Merrie had been her teacher. It was during those years when they had researched and learned about the benefits of plants.

"Aunt Florrie you were supposed to wait for us." Rory called to her Aunt who was busy setting the drying pans out on which they would place the wet seaweed to dry.

"Well I didn't know when you'd be coming so I thought I might as well get started."

Rory shook her head and hurried over to the garden shed to grab more drying pans. Aunt Florrie had always been a hard worker and usually got started quickly on most things. She kept them all organized so they got the work done.

Aunt Merrie followed and it didn't take long before they had ten long horizontal rows lined up.

Working together they pulled out buckets of seaweed out of the garden shed. They began sorting through the soggy long green plants laying them out on the drying pans.

She found a few tiny critters hiding in the long stemmed plants and used the garden hose to spray the plants clean.

"Rory, this is one of the largest piles of these slimy green plants you've harvested yet. You should be able to make a bunch of those skin care creams from this stack."

Aunt Florrie wrinkled her nose and sprayed the large plants she held tightly in her hands.

"What your aunt means to say is that we are very grateful for all your hard work researching and learning everything you have about these plants. You've managed to create skin creams that have helped each of us." Warmth flooded Rory as her gaze landed on Aunt Merrie's bright smile her cheeks now free of the rosacea that used to cover her nose and cheeks.

Her heart warmed knowing that all three Aunts had been helped by her plant mixtures. She wanted to do everything she could to help the three women who had raised her like surrogate moms after her parents died.

"You're welcome Auntie. I'm just happy we were able to learn about the helpful health benefits of all the green stuff in the sea."

Rory giggled as Aunt Florrie's hands got twisted up in the long green stems.

"There might be lots of health benefits but sometimes they are not so easy to handle." Aunt Florrie's shook her head as she struggled to untangle her hands.

"Let me help." Rory hurried to stand beside her aunt and helped unscramble her hands from the long strands of seaweed that clung together. When it was done she sprayed the last pile clean and set it on the drying pans. "All done. It should be dry by morning."

They took off their gloves and aprons they used for the dirty work and hung them up in the small porch by the back kitchen door.

Aunt Fawn had just finished setting the table when

they walked in the door. "Biscuits should be ready to eat by the time you all wash up."

Rory waited until Aunt Merrie and Aunt Florrie were finished. By the time she sat at the kitchen table her stomach had growled three times.

"Let's first give thanks." Aunt Fawn blessed the food and stood to ladle out the soup. "Rory dear, let me fill your bowl."

Once everyone was served the chatter began.

"Rory, tell us about your day. You must have found something interesting because you got home later than usual." Aunt Merrie buttered her biscuit one eyebrow tilted up in interest.

Her three aunts listened intently as Rory spoke. "I found an old wooden oar not far from the pier today. It might have been from that boating accident that was in Paradise Lake newspapers ten years ago."

"Maybe. Wouldn't that be interesting?" Aunt Florrie ladled more soup for herself and others.

"I also found a few sea critters trying to hide under rocks. Last night's strong winds must have brought the tide up and washed them ashore." Rory grinned always thrilled to see new things pop up on the beach.

"Did you get pictures?"

"Yes. Here they are." Rory opened her smartphone, scrolled to the pictures and passed her phone around the table. The smartphone she used was the same one her aunts gave her years ago. She took it with her everywhere to take pictures here on Walker's Island because they didn't have access to the Internet. "I'll print off this new collection of photos next time we go to Paradise Lake."

"We should get you another scrap book Rory. You've already filled the last one." Aunt Fawn loved pictures.

"Every once in awhile I go through your photo albums and scrap books. I was just looking at the pictures you took when we went sailing that last time with Walker Stevenson and his great-grandson Gabe. I think you were sixteen Rory. Too bad those days had to come to an end."

"As it turns out those days might not be completely at an end."

"Whatever do you mean Rory?" Aunt Fawn's eyebrows lifted in surprise.

"Just that I saw Gabe Stevenson today. He's back on the Island." All three aunts' eyes widened and their jaws dropped.

Rory grinned. "He wanted to see you all so I told him to stop by for lunch tomorrow."

❧

"Mommy where are you?" She woke up with a scream and sat straight up in bed panic squeezing her throat. Smoke filled the room and she could hardly breathe. Scurrying off her bed she ran from her room out into the hallway.

"Daddy?" Her hands shook as she ran them along the wall that led to her parents' bedroom. Fits of coughing soon followed. Where was Mommy? Why wasn't Daddy answering her? How come she could hardly breathe?

She called again only no one answered.

Sweat formed on her forehead as heat and flashes of fire spewed from the big crack in the door. She was about to touch the door when someone grabbed her by the shoulders and carried her away...

"Rory." In her nightmare she tried to shake the person off.

She was desperate to save her parents from the fire. "Rory wake up! We need your help!" Someone shook her shoulders once more and Rory opened her eyes wide. Aunt Florrie stood over her like an avenging angel.

She bolted upright somewhat taken aback by the shrill voice of her normally calm Aunt.

"What's happened? Are Aunt Merrie and Aunt Fawn okay?" Rory scrambled to get off the bed.

"Yes your aunts are fine. But, you'd better come outside." Without another word Aunt Florrie hurried out of her bedroom and ran down the stairs. Rory frowned and without bothering to change out of her pajamas chased after her down the stairs.

Flying out the door she was greeted by a haze of fire and smoke. Aunt Fawn had the water hose turned on high as she sprayed the hot house while Aunt Merrie threw water from overly full buckets onto the garden shed. Both small buildings had flames shooting out the sides.

"What happened?" Rory asked Aunt Florrie as she grabbed another bucket and filled it with water.

"We don't know. Both the seaweed and drying pans are ruined too. Sorry love." Her Aunt hurried to throw more water on the roof of the garden shed.

A truck door slammed and Rory turned to see Gabe running towards her. "I saw the smoke from the fire. Are you okay?"

"Yes. We're all okay. Just trying to put out the fire so it

doesn't reach the house." Rory handed him a bucket suddenly relieved to see Gabe.

"Let's form a line to get the water on the buildings faster." Gabe suggested and her aunts were eager to comply. After that, it didn't take long until they doused the fire.

Wide-eyed Rory stared at both small buildings where smoke and steam bounced off the rooftops. The hot house looked ready to collapse and the drying pans were all wrecked and the seaweed she'd harvested scattered and torn all over their back yard.

Tears filled her eyes and rolled down her cheeks clearing a path through the dirt and soot. She'd had so many plans to experiment with a new mixture of botanicals and plants and now most of it was doomed to lie in ashes.

"Sweetie we'll build again and it'll be even better next time you'll see." Aunt Merrie pulled her close and wrapped her in a big hug. Rory savored the comfort.

"I'll go make a pot of tea. It'll help settle our nerves as we figure out a way to solve this new problem." Aunt Florrie kissed her forehead and made her way into the house. Soon Aunt Merrie and Aunt Fawn followed.

"I'm sorry this happened Rory." Gabe spoke softly as he came to stand beside her. Rory did her best to wipe the tears off her cheeks before she looked up at him.

"Me too. I don't know what happened. All the tools I used were back in place and everything was in order before I went inside last night." Rory shivered and a furrow puckered her brows from anxiety. Huge knots of fear formed in her belly.

"I can tell you just thought of something. What is it?" Gabe tucked a long strand of hair behind her ear and Rory's heart fluttered at his touch.

He used to slip her hair behind her ears when they went sailing and would tell her he wanted to see her beautiful face. Today more than ever before, his gentle words and the warmth of his touch reached a place deep inside her heart.

It scared her how vulnerable she was to him.

Shifting from one foot to the other she looked away and swallowed, tamping down her emotions. Rory couldn't let Gabe see how much his nearness affected her.

She refocused and peered up at him unsure of how much to tell him. "To tell you the truth, there have been other strange things happening on the Island for the past year or so."

Gabe crossed his arms over his chest. "What? What do you mean by strange things?"

Rory shifted her feet. "Just human footprints from our house through the trees to the beach that were not from us. And little things like the greenhouse herbs being ruined and someone smashing all my jars that I use for making my skin care creams."

Gabe's lips formed a thin line a tick appearing along his jawline. "Exactly when were you going to tell me?"

"Honestly Gabe you don't need to get so upset. We thought it was a small thing. And besides where would we have found you to tell you anything?"

Her tone of voice was sharper than she intended. This show of emotion on her part surprised even her.

Maybe it was time for her to admit that it really bothered her that he'd left suddenly almost five years ago. She knew he was busy with his speaking and training events. But she thought they had become friends. True friends kept in touch.

Why did Gabe expect to be informed of these strange incidents when he hadn't cared enough to talk to her in years?

He expelled a breath and ran a hand through his hair. "You're right. I haven't done much to earn the right to know what's going on in your life. I've done a terrible job at keeping in touch." Her eyes widened that he'd read her mind. For a moment it seemed like time stood still. They could still read each other's thoughts from all those summers spent together.

"I'm sorry Rory. I'm going to do better. I'll do whatever it takes so you and your aunts are safe. Forgive me?"

"Sure. Of course I forgive you." Rory said quickly. She could admit she was still a little peaked at him but her heart softened at his heartfelt apology.

Turmoil stirred in her belly.

She bit her lip to stop herself from crying as her gaze swept over the devastation and ashes in their backyard. Why did this happen to them?

Gabe reached for her hand and squeezed it gently. She closed her eyes and sighed.

Hopelessness washed over her.

He rubbed the top of her hand with his thumb. "We're going to find a way to protect all of you, I promise."

"Thanks Gabe. I know you mean well but how do we know when or how this person will strike again? From what I can see the problem is that whoever is doing this seems to be targeting me specifically." Her forehead puckered with worry before she looked up at him. "For some reason they want to ruin anything that is near or dear to me. I'm so scared this person will hurt my Aunts."

Gabe put one arm around her shoulders for a moment and whispered. "Not on my watch."

Rory shivered with warmth at his unexpected embrace. His arm trembled slightly and he kissed the top of her head.

She was surprised at the swiftness and intensity of his protectiveness. Without warning, memories flitted across her mind of that country song Gabe sang each time he took her out on his sailboat. *Cowboy Take Me Away* by the country band Dixie Chicks.

He'd caught her singing and dancing to that song one summer when she was thirteen and had teased her with it ever since.

Her heart turned to mush whenever she remembered those few weeks every summer she spent with him.

Being so close to Gabe Stevenson, the man she'd dreamed about for years, made her long for more.

She just wanted to be close to him. Everyday.

Rory shut out that thought as quickly as it came. She couldn't afford to let herself be drawn in by this man. Gabe was someone who was famous and in demand. He would forever be out of her reach.

She needed to guard her heart. *Don't let yourself fall for him. He will always be a man who spends time with you and just as suddenly leaves you again.*

With that sober reminder Rory stepped out of his reach nervously running a hand through her messy hair.

"I think this is a problem that won't be fixed in one day. Let's go inside and have some of Aunt Florrie's tea."

Gabe nodded his face pensive. "Sounds good. And I am going to have a talk with your aunts. We've got to figure out a way to solve this."

Rory nodded as she turned and opened the kitchen door. She saw all three aunts sitting and talking around the table.

"We thought we'd join you three for tea." Rory pulled a chair out for Gabe. "But first I'm going to wash off this soot and dirt. Be back soon."

Rory hurried up the stairs to her room and took a quick shower changing into clean jeans and a t-shirt. Brushing out her hair she quickly put it up in a ponytail.

As she hurried back down the stairs she heard Aunt Merrie speaking in hushed whispers but Rory couldn't hear what they were saying.

Gabe pulled out a letter from his pocket as soon as she sat at the table. "This is the letter Grand told me to give you. Sorry it took me awhile to bring it to you."

Aunt Merrie read the letter from Walker Stevenson out loud: *To my three good fairies. If you're reading this I've gone on to my reward. I want to tell you one last time how much I appreciate the three of you gals for how you saved my neck all those years ago. You did me a good turn and now I want to repay the favor.*

All three of you and your beautiful niece Rory need better access in case things take a turn for the worse on that Island. So, I thought I'd pull out one last trick I have hidden up my sleeve - - surprised you didn't I?

I've given instructions to my old lawyer and his son that as soon as you give him this letter they will set up Satellite to the Island so that you have Internet access. I should have done it years ago but never got around to it. Now it'll get done.

My great-grandson Gabe will help out with anything else you need, tell him Grand said so. My hope is that these new services will help you all feel safer, more connected to others and more at peace on the Island. I hope you enjoy that little slice of heaven on earth as much as I have. Walker Stevenson.

Rory looked around the table and saw all three of her aunts dabbing at their eyes. "It's just like your great-grandfather to do something crazy and wonderful like this as a last surprise." Aunt Merrie's eyelashes glistened with tears as she looked over at Gabe.

"Yeah, he always did like surprising people by having the last word." Gabe chuckled softly. Rory could tell he was moved by his great-grandfather's kind gesture too. "Well I'm glad Grand did this. I'll need to go to Seattle to get that satellite setup as well as take care of a few things. I hope to be back on the Island by the end of the week." He nodded to everyone and walked to the door.

Rory followed him outside.

"It was thoughtful of your great-grandfather to do that for us. We'll all feel safer for it." Rory stood with her hands tucked in her pockets looking down at her feet before meeting Gabe's gaze.

He grinned and a crinkle formed along the edge of his mesmerizing blue eyes. "Grand always loved his surprises. It's just like him to have one last hurrah."

Memories of summers spent laughing at Walker Stevenson's teasing rose to the surface.

Rory treasured those days.

Gabe reached over and tucked a strand of blond hair behind one ear. Rory shivered at his touch. "Grand really cared about his four Island ladies. He wanted you to have fun and feel safe here."

She swallowed back tears. There hadn't been many people in their lives who had cared what happened to the four of them. It had been the four of them doing so much of life alone ever since she was a little girl. A painful longing squeezed her belly at Gabe's touch.

Rory forced it down and blinked rapidly trying desperately to hold back tears that threatened to spill over.

"Well I should get going." Gabe squeezed her hand. "I'll be back Friday. We can go sailing then."

She forced a smile and waved as he got in Grand's old truck and drove away.

As the truck disappeared behind the trees a familiar pain pierced her heart.

Gabe had left.

She was grateful he was making their Island a safer place, but in some ways she wished he would disappear out of their lives again.

It was too painful to have Gabe close by only to have him leave again. It was too difficult to be reminded of her attraction to him everyday.

Besides what if they really weren't safe here?

Her aunts had told her on her eighteenth birthday that someone they knew a long time ago had threatened to harm her when she turned twenty-one. So every year when the calendar moved closer to her birthday her aunts insisted she stay close to home.

Rory trembled at the reminder. Her birthday was very soon.

She would need to make sure Gabe was far away from her on that day. Rory was terrified somehow he would be harmed. She would do everything possible so no one else she loved was hurt.

Pushing her shoulders back she walked into the cottage with a new resolve.

No matter which way I look at it, I'd best not let myself get too attached to Gabe Stevenson.

If I do, it'll mean trouble for both of us.

CHAPTER THREE

abe

"Where to Mr. Stevenson?" Gabe had just settled his yacht at his friend Dan's Seattle Marina when his limo driver drove up and opened the door for him.

"I have an appointment with Grand's lawyer down-town. Thanks Henry." Gabe sat down in the limo resting his head against the headrest as the car drove away.

His thoughts returned to what Rory's Aunts had hurriedly whispered in his ear this morning while their niece had been upstairs changing her clothes.

"I'm afraid all this trouble might have come to us because of Rory's past." Aunt Fawn started to tell him the story a solemn expression in her grey eyes.

"You see before Rory was born her father had a mistress.

He'd convinced Rory's mom he loved her, but his actions proved otherwise. Maybe the mistress is trying somehow to get back at our Rory? We also have an older sister - Rory's Aunt Mallory.

Last time she saw Rory was when she was five years old, I believe. Mal always told Delanie that she spoiled the little princess too much. Mal complained that Rory got everything that should have come to Mal, but never did. But we haven't heard from Mal for a long time so I don't think there's anything to worry about there.

Aunt Florrie sighed heavily and looked at Gabe. "We don't know for certain if someone is trying to harm her. But will you look into this and help us find a way to protect our niece?"

"And without telling her about this conversation?" Aunt Merrie added.

Gabe of course had agreed.

His thoughts were still whirling when Henry opened the car door.

"We're here sir."

Startled Gabe expelled a breath and gathered his brief-case. "I'm on my way. Thanks, Henry."

He looked up at the old brick building. Large box-style gold letters of *Sterling and Sons* hung stately on the front of the building giving the law office the impression of a resilient strength. It reminded him of Grand.

Walking up the front steps he remembered every Christmas Grand gave a gift to Robert Sterling as a way of showing appreciation for all he did. They had been long time friends and Grand had trusted Mr. Sterling implicitly.

Gabe introduced himself to the receptionist who sent a quick message to her boss.

She stood to her feet. "Mr. Sterling will see you now. Please follow me." Gabe followed the woman to a large office and was promptly greeted by the lawyer himself.

Grand's old lawyer now had a completely white head of hair and more wrinkles on his face than Gabe remembered. He shook his hand a large grin on his face. "Gabe Stevenson. Always happy to have a member of Walker Stevenson's family in my office."

"Mr. Sterling thanks for seeing me. You're doing well?"

"Still alive and kicking so that's something." Mr. Sterling gestured for him to sit down and went to sit behind his desk. "What brings you here today, Gabe?"

Gabe expelled a heavy sigh and began to tell him about Grand's letter and the incidents that had been going on near the cottage. "Rory and her three aunts are really looking forward to having the satellite set up around their cottage on Walker's Island."

"Ah, yes. I remember the day Walker came to my office and let me know about his plans. I thought he had some good ideas. Still do. I'll ask my son Steven to do the legwork on this. We'll get this in motion this week."

"That's a weight off my mind." Gabe expelled a breath. "My plan is to move to the Island for a few weeks. I'm also looking to hire a team to set up hidden security cameras on the Island. I'll sleep better at night knowing those are in place."

Mr. Sterling eyed him for a moment before searching through his business cards. "If you want someone you can trust to setup the security cameras and uncover who is behind the trouble on the Island, Max Harrington is your man. He's a former Navy Seal who now does his own work as a private investigator. He has a team of veterans who are very thorough. I've hired his team myself. Max can be trusted to be discreet."

Gabe took the business card from Mr. Sterling. "This is just what I need. I'll set up an appointment with him and see what he can do." He stood up and shook the old lawyer's hand. "Now I know why Grand trusted you with so much Mr. Sterling. Thank you."

"Just happy to help one of Walker's family. Speaking of your great-grandfather and his plans, is there to be a Mrs. Gabe Stevenson in the near future?" Mr. Sterling walked him to the door a big grin on his face.

"I'm hoping there will be." Gabe hesitated and shook his head with a half smile. He surprised himself in that moment realizing it was true. "I'll send you and Mrs. Sterling an invitation when I know for sure."

"You do that my boy! We'll be there. Then I can give you the deed of ownership for Walker's Island." Mr. Sterling clapped him on the back.

"That sounds really good. Thanks again, Mr. Sterling." Gabe chuckled and shook his hand before hurrying out to his waiting limo.

He laughed a little as he thought of what he'd just told Grand's old lawyer. *There might be a Mrs. Gabe Stevenson in the near future? That's the first time he'd said that out loud and thought of a woman he would really like to wear that title. A certain blond haired Island beauty who was part imp and part mermaid came to mind.*

Gabe shook his head. Was he really thinking of doing this? He would only do this to lay claim to Walker's Island. He was not going to allow himself to be in the position to be vulnerable to anyone else. Memories of what happened to his Dad returned in full force.

No, he would need to keep his emotions under control and make this strictly a marriage of convenience.

Before Gabe took the leap, he really needed to talk to someone he respected.

As Henry dropped him off at his Condo Gabe thought of Cyrus Noble's charity event tonight.

Maybe he should find a moment to get advice from Adam or Jack.

His older brothers had already been through this. He trusted them to help steer him in the right direction.

JAZZ MUSIC FILLED the air with sultry, soft tones as Gabe walked into the massive ballroom of *The Noble Seascape Hotel*.

It was one of the most elegant hotels in Seattle. This place was close to the waterfront and the beautiful view drew visitors from all over the world.

Gabe adjusted the front of his tuxedo already eager to get out of his penguin suit. But that would have to wait.

Looking around the room, he spotted his friend from college. Dan Summers. He'd been friends with Dan's older brother Billy years ago. When Billy died Gabe started befriending Danny and they had continued to stay in touch with each other ever since.

Dan stood near the water fountain and waved him over.

"Hey man it's good to see you." Dan grabbed his hand a grin on his face.

"Good to see you too Dan. How's the Marina business going?" Gabe had always thought it ideal that Dan's father had been able to use their family name to their advantage. *Summers Seaside Marina* was a popular destination for residents and tourists alike.

"It's going well. I'm busier than ever. Dad wants to retire so he can take mom travelling. Looks like I'll be taking over the company soon." His friend shrugged. "I guess it's time for me to step up to family responsibility."

"That's good. You and Amy planning on getting married any time soon?" Gabe remembered Dan's girlfriend from college and how perfect Amy seemed for him.

"We're planning a Christmas wedding as we speak." Dan's gaze narrowed as if trying to draw out Gabe's secrets. "Speaking of getting married, I loved watching Winny O quiz you on your love life in that recent interview."

Gabe grimaced as his friend chuckled. "Yeah, that was uncomfortable to say the least."

"Yet you won over the audience anyway. You were great. So, is it true that you need to marry soon to get your great-grandfather's inheritance?"

"Sadly yes. I'm still undecided if I'll take on that challenge or not." Gabe rubbed the back of his neck.

"I think you should. It's a beautiful Island." Dan looked over his shoulder for moment and grimaced speaking in a half whisper. "Only make sure you choose the right woman. Maddie seems eager for the position. She's walking this way."

"What?" Gabe's stomach lurched as he turned to see his old girlfriend making her way toward him.

Dan looked at him with a better-you-than-me sardonic grin. "Have fun. See you later." His friend walked away before Gabe could find a reason for him to stay.

He really didn't want to talk to Maddie. As she drew nearer he caught a glimpse of a low cut red evening gown with a slit that was cut high up to her thighs.

Gabe quickly moved his gaze up to her face. Her green eyes were pouty and flirty just like the rest of her.

Her sparkling jewels and glittering makeup had always seemed overdone. It didn't appeal to him. Suddenly an image of Rory wearing shorts and a t-shirt walking along the beach formed in his mind. To him Rory was more beautiful in her natural state than Maddie or any of the women here tonight.

Where did that thought come from?

No sooner had he tamped those thoughts down than Maddie appeared at his side.

"Gabe Stevenson, I never doubted I'd find you here tonight." Maddie stood near him and slipped one hand into the curve of his arm as if she belonged there. "You always seem to show up at these charity events. I guess it's good for your image so why not?" She looked up at him a flirtatious smile on her face.

"Maddie you're mistaken. I only show up for causes I believe in, not because I want to look good." Irritated Gabe started to step away from her.

Before he could pull his arm away the flash of a nearby camera nearly blinded him. He looked in front of them and saw a cameraman trying to get another picture of them.

Gabe pulled his arm away from Maddie and quickly showed his back to the cameraman.

"What's wrong Gabe? Are you suddenly shy of the camera?" Maddie persisted.

His brows puckered in frustration as he turned to look at her. "Honestly? I do get tired of being constantly in the spotlight."

Looking down at her he could see a spark of confusion. "I would never get tired of being in front of the camera."

And therein lay the difference between them.

When he was in front of the camera it was from an effort to help people discover their best self and to help them break off limitations so they could get ahead in life. For Maddie it seemed her sole purpose was to show her face and figure for the world to admire.

Gabe bit back his frustration and instead asked pointedly, "Maddie what do you want?"

"Why, I just wanted to say hi. I knew you would be here tonight and I thought maybe we could get together after the event. You know we could catch up for old times sake." Her lips formed a teasing pout that many men had fallen for including him.

Not this time.

"Sorry, but I must decline Maddie. We already talked about this. I'm not interested in getting back together." Gabe was about to say more when suddenly the Master of Ceremonies walked up to the microphone.

"Ladies and gentlemen if you could all take your seats we'll be starting soon. Thank you."

"Looks like that's my cue. As always it's been interesting Maddie." Gabe rescued his arm from her grip.

Her brows furrowed in frustration and he heard the click-clack of her designer shoe tapping a steady rhythm on the ballroom floor. "You should rethink your decision Gabe. You might be sorry you ever let me go."

"I don't think so Maddie. Enjoy your evening." Gabe stepped back and with a curt nod walked away.

Looking over the large crowd mixed with designer dresses and tuxedos he spotted Cyrus Noble talking with his brother Jack. Gabe joined them as they walked toward the table nearest the stage.

"Well if it isn't Gabe Stevenson." Cyrus grabbed his hand and pulled him into a massive bear hug. Gabe couldn't help but grin as he was swallowed up in the strong arms of this giant of a man.

Cyrus Noble was as mammoth in size as was his billionaire dollar chain of luxury hotels. Cyrus released his hold on Gabe, slapped his back with a big grin and turned to speak to his wife. "Anna, look what the cat dragged in."

They had reached a large table where Cyrus's wife Anna stood talking with Jack's wife Bella and Adam's wife Elle.

"Gabriel Stevenson how nice that you've joined us." Anna Noble was much smaller than her husband and was as classy as her husband was unrefined. She pulled him into a soft hug and then with one hand tapped the seat beside her. "Come sit on my other side and tell me what you've been up to lately."

He grinned and accepted Anna's kind invitation. It was nice to sit at the same table with this older couple he so admired.

Anna and Cyrus were opposites but were so in love with each other that all you could see were how well they completed each other. Gabe saw Cyrus as a father figure and mentor. He'd come to appreciate his advice in many areas of life and business.

Cyrus leaned down, kissed his wife's cheek and held the chair out for her. Anna sat down gracefully and started up the conversation.

"It's so nice to share a meal with the Stevenson brothers and their wives tonight. To friends." Anna raised her glass and they all joined in the toast. "So Gabriel tell me what you're up to."

Gabe leaned back and began to tell Anna about the many different events he had spoken at and the positive response from the audiences.

"Sounds like you're having a real impact. That doesn't surprise me." Anna's gentle smile of appreciation warmed his heart and reminded him of his Mom. She was his biggest supporter. "What is surprising to me is why you're not married yet. Gabriel, you are a fine catch for any woman. Your two brothers are blissfully enjoying the married state, yet you're here without a woman on your arm. Why is that?"

Both Adam and Jack grinned at him from across the table. Gabe squirmed in his chair. He didn't like it when the focus fell on him especially around the topic of marriage. Both of his brothers had their arms around their wives enjoying this conversation a little too much.

"I guess I haven't found a woman I love enough to marry yet." Gabe took a long sip of water hoping the topic would soon switch to something else.

Cyrus set down his drink and spoke up. "Anna love, didn't you watch Winny O's interview with Gabe? He told the world that he has to marry by his birthday or lose the inheritance from his great-grandfather."

Anna looked at her husband before turning back to Gabe. "Sorry, I didn't see the interview. So what do you inherit from your great-grandfather if you marry by your birthday?"

"I'll get Walker's Island. It's a beautiful Island of about ten square miles that is basically untouched. It's beautiful."

"You have plans for it?" Cyrus raised a curious eyebrow.

Gabe nodded. "I do. I was thinking I would take one half of the Island and make it into a Resort. It would be a place where people could come for the health spa, but it would also be a place that would go hand-in-glove as an incentive for my personal development training. I'm still flushing out ideas, but I think it has real potential."

"Hmm, that is a good idea Gabe."

"Once you have it built we'll be one of your first customers." Anna smiled and winked. "That's good that you have your goals laid out clearly. I'm sure it won't be long now until you're happily married."

"Watch out Gabe. It's my wife's mission in life to see everyone she knows happily married." Cyrus chuckled as he squeezed his wife's hand. "But on a more serious note here's some fatherly advice. You'll know when you've met the woman you love because you won't be able to get through one day without thinking about her and doing everything in your power to make her happy. When you meet her, don't wait. Marry her and make her yours. That's what I did and it changed my life."

Cyrus kissed his wife's hand and she smiled adoringly at her husband.

"Thanks Cyrus. I appreciate the advice." Gabe nodded shifting in his seat as one finger traced the bottom of his water glass.

"I think we're making Gabe uncomfortable Cyrus." Anna looked at her husband. He grinned.

"You may be right. We can switch to another topic. I do have an idea I want to run by you Gabe." Cyrus waited until the waiter set the dessert and coffee around the table.

While everyone was enjoying dessert Cyrus spoke again. "I wanted to ask if you'd be willing to be my keynote speaker for the conference I've scheduled for the managers and employees of the Noble Hotel chain."

Gabe stared at him for a full minute before answering. This was something he had only dreamed about, never thinking that Cyrus Noble would actually ask him to speak at one of his hotel conferences.

"Gabe, what do you say?"

"I'm truly honored that you would ask me Cyrus. Speaking at one of your conferences would be incredible. That's something I've always wanted to do but never thought I'd get the chance." Gabe grinned at his mentor.

"Good, good. I'm glad we'll be working together son.

I'll get you the dates of the next set of conferences as soon as my conference manager has them confirmed." Cyrus nodded and turned to talk to his brothers at the table.

Gabe's head was still spinning, excited at working closely with Cyrus Noble. His mind whirled even as the speaker stood at the podium began to address the crowd.

When the speaker finished, Cyrus and Anna were immediately surrounded by a crowd of people. Gabe said his goodbyes and walked toward the exit with his brothers and their wives.

"It was great to talk with Cyrus and Anna tonight." Gabe looked up at Jack who wore a strange expression on his face. It seemed like he was deeply pondering something. "I was slightly uncomfortable with all the questions about finding a wife but that's okay I'm getting used to it."

"So, have you found a woman to marry?" Jack questioned.

"I'm not sure." Gabe stood beside Jack and loosened his bow tie as they waited for their limousine drivers to arrive. "There's one woman I'm attracted to more than any other. Since my birthday is coming rather quickly, I'm thinking about following in your footsteps. Maybe a marriage-of-convenience is what I need to do to get my inheritance. It worked for you and Adam."

"True. But take it from me. You need to figure out what she really needs so she'll agree to marry you." Jack studied him with those probing hazel eyes. Gabe pondered his words realizing the one thing Rory needed more than anything was to move out of that cottage so she'd be safe.

Gabe rubbed his jaw. Maybe he could convince Rory

she needed him as much as he needed her. He only hoped she would see it the same way he did.

Jack's pirate smile was back in full force. "Gabe you have the same look as you did when you'd win against Dad in one of those pinewood racing car tournaments years ago."

"Yeah. It feels about the same." Gabe felt that familiar flutter of warmth. He was getting ready to win, big time.

His limo driver arrived and Gabe quickly pulled Jack into a quick hug. "Thanks, Jack. I needed that." He quickly hugged Bella, Elle and Adam and hurried out to the waiting car.

It looked like he had a few things to take care of before he went back to Walker's Island.

He only hoped Rory would agree to his plan.

CHAPTER FOUR

ory

ARIANNA ROMANO STOOD behind the counter of her family's bakery, looking at the clock on the wall. It was almost eight in the morning. Soon he would be here.

For the past three weeks ever since he had moved back to their small town, Jared Berkley stopped by every weekday morning to get half a dozen muffins.

He was the guy in High School whom she'd always dreamed of dating, but nothing had ever happened. It didn't help that Jared was three years older and that he'd come from the right side of the tracks where the wealthy families lived.

She had always lived on the poor side of the town. Jared and her didn't have any friends or anything else in common.

In fact Arianna was quite convinced Jared didn't even know she existed.

He'd left town to go to college. But six years later, he'd started a coffee shop franchise and suddenly moved back to their small town.

The best news was that he had come back single.

She hoped she would get to serve him again today.

"Arianna please clean table number five." Her papa a proud Italian man, was a stickler for cleanliness in their family-owned bakery. Her parents had moved years ago to this small town to start their business. Arianna was their only child as the doctor told her mama she couldn't have any more children. It was just the three of them running their small bakery and coffee shop. She noticed her parents needed her help more and more each year they grew older.

"Yes Papa." Arianna hurried to find the disinfectant and clean cloth and walked over to the row of tables near the front window. Wiping the napkin holder and the salt and pepper shaker her thoughts were so filled with the handsome blonde and blue-eyed man that she accidentally dropped the glass pepper shaker to the floor.

"Oh no." She stooped down and grabbed a couple of napkins from her pocket. Reaching down to the linoleum floor, she began to clean up the shattered glass.

"Allow me." A deep voice whispered and a large hand covered hers.

Startled Arianna turned her head to look into the deepest blue eyes she'd ever seen. Here was the same man she had day dreamed about kissing her. Almost as if he could read her thoughts, his gaze moved downward to her lips. Arianna caught her breath anticipating the sweetness of his lips on hers...

A loud bark shattered the silence.

It was jarring to suddenly switch from writing a scene

where Gabe — or the hero of her romance Jared — had almost kissed the heroine only to be interrupted by a dog.

Rory stopped typing and quickly set her laptop down on the cushioned window seat in her bedroom. She turned to see her brown Labrador dog run from the door and jump onto the soft seat beside her. Following close behind as usual was his playmate.

"Mocha, hush." Rory scolded the brown lab and sternly eyed the golden haired lab beside him. "You too, Latte. Their tails wagged as their big round eyes stared out the window at the scene below.

Rory turned to see what they were looking at.

Her lips formed a large smile as she saw the men carrying the ladder and leftover cable back to their truck.

It looked like they had finished installing the satellite. One of the guys who installed it had shown her how to set it up so she could access the Internet.

She grabbed her computer and was soon signed in and able to email her friend.

Hey Raz. Can meet tomorrow for lunch? Aunt Merrie and I will be coming to Paradise Lake.

It didn't take long before Raz replied.

I'd love to. Meet me at the gift shop and we'll go for lunch.

Great! I'll see you then.

THE NEXT MORNING Rory's alarm went off early. She hurried through the shower.

By the time she got downstairs Aunt Florrie was already bustling around in the kitchen.

"Sorry I'm running behind. I'll just grab a toast." Rory kissed her Aunt's cheek.

"Already done. I heard you running around upstairs and I made toast for you."

"Thanks Auntie."

Aunt Merrie fluttered into the room and soon they were both eating.

"Here's the list of groceries and other supplies." Aunt Florrie handed a long list to her sister.

Aunt Fawn slowly walked into the kitchen leaning heavily on her cane.

"Let me help you Aunt Fawn." She pulled out the chair and helped her aunt to sit down.

"You're a good girl Rory." Her Aunt expelled a low groan as she sat down. Rory brought a cup of coffee to her. "Thank you."

"You're welcome. Take it easy today while we're gone, okay?"

Aunt Fawn simply nodded a pained look on her pale face.

Rory and Aunt Merrie slipped their jackets on and with a last goodbye hurried outside and toward the pier where the boat would meet them.

They hurried down the familiar trail between the trees that led to the beach where Walker Stevenson had built his long pier. Sure enough the orange and white boat waited for them.

Jerry Waterman the captain, stood at the helm of the small ferry that held eight cars and fifty passengers. He waved at them and they hurried onto the boat.

The motors rumbled and the boat gained speed. Rory

loved watching the ripples of water as they moved faster. She'd done this since she was six years old and never got tired of it.

"It sure was good of Walker Stevenson to plan all those years ago for us to have a weekly boat service from the Island to Paradise Lake."

Aunt Merrie nodded. "He sure did take good care of us. Even now that he's passed away he's continued to see to our needs. He was a good man." A secret smile lit up her Aunt's face. "And so is his great-grandson Gabe."

Heat curled in her belly stretching upwards to her neck warming her cheeks. "I know. But before you get any ideas we're just friends."

"Hmm." Rory grimaced at Aunt Merrie's noncommittal response. She realized her Aunt didn't believe a word of it.

Rory silently shook her head knowing it was useless to argue. Didn't Aunt Merrie realize Gabe Stevenson was way out of her league? He was a billionaire who was well known across the nation. Not only that but he only saw her as a younger sister.

She on the other hand had been raised on a small Island with her three aunts and had only ever been to Paradise Lake and Seattle. Her poor girl status wasn't even in the same ballpark as Gabe's wealth. No she was sure all they could be was friends.

Why then did she still wish for more?

As the ferry neared the Paradise Lake docks Rory did her best to shake off the sudden gloom that descended on her.

They stepped off the boat and Rory straightened her shoulders as they hurried toward the waiting taxi. She was determined today would be a good day and a wonderful visit with her best friend.

The taxi took them to main-street where Aunt Merrie got out to do her shopping. "I'll meet you back here in four hours."

"I'll be here. Thanks Auntie." Rory waved at her aunt and gave the driver directions to her friend Raz's house.

The car stopped in front of a two-story house that was on the corner of main-street on the southern side of Paradise Lake. The bottom half of the house was a gift and coffee shop while the top half was where Razelle lived with her mother. Their house and business was located near the highway, which meant more people stopped by.

Rory paid the driver and entered the gift shop. Raz was busy wrapping a gift for a customer so she walked around the shop exploring all the imported and rare items.

"You came. I'm so glad to see you." Raz threw her arms around her.

Rory always felt so special when her friend greeted her so enthusiastically. She was outgoing and bubbly while Rory was quiet and subdued. In many ways they were opposites. Sometimes Rory wished she could be more like her friend.

Stepping back, Rory gazed into her friend's sea green eyes framed by dark brown eyebrows and eyelashes. Her long hair that her mother had forbidden her to cut, hung down past her hips in a thick reddish-brown braid.

"I did. I'm so happy to see you."

"I'm glad to see you too. Wait here and I'll take a minute to give Luella some instructions so we can visit for a couple hours without interruption." Raz went to talk with another woman who was busy taking gift items out of boxes.

"There. Now let's go to the coffee shop and we can have lunch there. Sorry, I wish we could go somewhere else today but Mother insisted I stay nearby in case she needs me." Her friend lifted her shoulders in a helpless shrug.

"That's okay. I understand." Rory could understand about having protective parents. After all her three aunts were like three watchful parents who had hovered over her since she was six years old.

They walked into the coffee shop and Raz made a beeline for the table in the far corner. "If we sit here at least we have a little more privacy."

"Sounds good."

They ordered a simple lunch of finger food. When Raz's mother brought the food over she didn't seem happy. "Here you go. I think you need to get back at it as soon as you finish eating Razelle."

"But mother you promised me two hours with Rory unless there was an emergency."

Her friend's mother hesitated for a moment. Finally she sighed. "Oh all right. But then you should go upstairs after you have lunch so my customers don't see you sitting around. I really don't want my customers thinking my daughter is lazy."

"We'll go to the apartment right after we finish eating." Raz promised.

Her friend's mom walked away. Before long they had finished their food and were hurrying up the stairs.

On entering Raz's bedroom in their two bedroom upstairs apartment Rory set her shoulder bag down and sank down on the bed. Her friend's white cat Sunbeam hopped on the bed wanting to play.

"Hey fluffy kitty." The cat was soon purring as Rory scratched Sunbeam's belly.

"So Rory tell me everything that's been happening with you? Your message sounded a little mysterious."

Rory had been friends with Raz ever since they'd started music and swimming lessons together at seven years of age. Her aunts had sacrificed so much just so she could take lessons and get to know other kids her age.

Raz and Rory saw each other every week for that year of lessons and they continued to grow closer to become the best of friends.

So when Rory sent her a message Raz was eager for a visit.

"I guess it sounded that way. So much has been happening these past few weeks and I wanted to talk to you." Rory went on to tell her friend about the unexpected fire and how it had destroyed all her hard work.

"Oh I'm so sorry. Especially after all the work you've done."

"Yes it's been very difficult. Now I don't know how I'm going to get all the tools and plants setup in time for the upcoming end of summer town festival. But I've already promised. Somehow I need to get more plants harvested and mix together for my skin care creams. The problem is that I don't have enough sea plants. I need large quantities and I only have three weeks to find it. I'm afraid there might not be a way to get what I need in time."

"Maybe you should make a list of everything you need and brainstorm solutions for each item."

Rory nodded. "That would help."

"So you got the fire out and everyone's okay?"

"Yes, thank God. Gabe Stevenson showed up unexpectedly to help. He said something about doing what he could to make Walker's Island safe for us."

Raz eyed her for a moment. "That's good." Her best friend grinned. "Hmm, so that's why you have a new sparkle in your eyes."

Heat crept up Rory's neck to her cheeks. "Maybe I'm just grateful for his help."

"Yeah right. Don't forget I've seen how sad and gloomy you've been every summer after Gabe Stevenson left Walker's Island." Raz teased.

Her friend knew her well.

"I just miss his company. Gabe's a good friend. And he only sees me as his little sister."

Raz laughed out loud. "Have you looked in the mirror lately? You're beautiful. You have curves in all the right places and you are kind and generous. You are not his sister and I'm sure by now he's realized that."

The corners of her mouth lifted a little at her friend's encouraging words. "Well, I don't think he sees me that way." Rory sighed.

"Anyway, I'm not going to think about that. My biggest concern right now is how to keep my aunts safe from whoever is doing these strange things on the Island. Also I need to figure out how to get my skin care back up and running now that I've lost my supplies."

Raz leaned over and squeezed her hand gently. "It'll work out. I'm confident of that."

"Maybe." Rory looked at her watch. "I need to be going. Aunt Merrie will be waiting. Thanks for taking time out of your busy day to chat."

"Anytime. Especially if you want to talk about your love interest."

Rory folded her arms across her chest rolling her eyes when her best friend wagged her eyebrows suggestively.

Walking to the door she spoke softly. "We'll see what happens. But right now, I'm going to focus on how to keep my aunts safe and figure out a way to get large amounts of sea plants that I desperately need."

Rory thought about their conversation as they returned to the Island.

SLINGING the beach towel over her shoulder and clutching her tote bag in the one hand she tilted her head upwards enjoying the warmth of the morning sun.

Rory's thoughts lingered on the conversation with Raz yesterday.

She had already spent the morning hand picking more seaweed and setting it on makeshift wooden boards. It was a new way of doing things and she didn't mind experimenting. But at this slow rate she would never have what she needed in time.

However, she still needed proper containers and more botanical oils. Tonight she would research online. Now that they had access to Satellite Internet on the Island research would be a much simpler process.

For today however her aunts told her to take a break. She decided to go to the beach. It was a sunny day and the thought of spending a little more time outside in the fresh air felt wonderful.

Mocha and Latte trotted next to her acting as guards. Ever since the fire she took the dogs with her wherever she went. Her Aunt Florrie had insisted on the dogs and that she always took her two-way walkie-talkie with her.

Anxiety weighed heavy on her shoulders like a massive bag of wet sea plants but she refused to stay confined to the house because of fear.

Besides, she'd reminded her aunts that whoever was behind the scare tactics seemed to do their evil deeds after dark.

Still she would feel better when Gabe returned to the Island. Maybe he would have a strategy to help keep them safe.

Staring at the long stretch of water in front of her, Rory wished she could see Gabe's yacht, but it was nowhere in sight. Instead, she spotted several boats moving across the water headed to other Islands. Most likely it was tourists enjoying some time on the waterway.

The only person missing to make this day great was Gabe.

Rory let out a long sigh as she walked along the beach. She stopped when she came to her favorite spot.

With one hand shielding her eyes from the sun, she looked up at the tall sturdy oak tree. This was the very tree where her and Gabe had carved their names when she was sixteen.

With one finger she traced the makeshift scribbles they'd etched into the wood. She smiled softly as memories surfaced of Gabe covering his much larger hand over hers and carving their names into this tree together.

Rory flexed her hand even now as familiar warm tingles began in her hand and spread to her whole body.

That summer had been the first time her awareness had shifted and she became aware of Gabe as man. No longer had she seen him as her big brother. It was also the summer he'd left the Island almost as quickly as he came.

After that summer she couldn't stop thinking about Gabe Stevenson. It seemed like memories surrounded her wherever she went on the Island. Even her night dreams were filled with Gabe.

After that, Rory began to write her first romance. The love stories poured out of her. Some scenes were shaped from memories but all the stories were inspired from what she imagined it would be like to be loved by a man like Gabe Stevenson.

Expelling a breath, she turned to set her tote bag against the base of the tree.

Laying the beach towel on the sand she pulled out her manuscript and pen from the tote bag. She was now writing her tenth novel and it had all begun with Gabe.

She had him to thank for being her inspiration.

The corners of her lips turned up and she began to read what she'd written so far in her latest romance. Lying down on her large beach towel she read through the first few chapters using her red pen to cross things off and make the needed changes.

Soon the warmth of the sun made her a little sleepy. She put her manuscript down and set a rock on top of the pages so they wouldn't fly away. Quickly shedding her oversized t-shirt to the blue spaghetti strap shirt she wore underneath she decided to give herself a little time to tan. For just a little while she would close her eyes.

Soon she was dreaming that Gabe had returned to the Island. His loud familiar whistle seemed so real.

A scrunching and rustling of papers woke her up.

Her eyes flew open and her heart rate accelerated in fear. Was someone trying to sneak up on her?

Squinting from the bright sun Rory shielded her eyes surprised when she saw Gabe.

She expelled a quick breath. What was he doing picking up papers that were scattered across the beach? He whistled as he went.

Her two dogs followed at his heels like he was the *Pied Piper*. Where was their loyalty? *Traitors.*

By the time Rory sat up he was walking her way.

Gabe squatted beside her the large stack of papers swishing in his hands.

Rory rubbed her eyes trying to make sure she wasn't still dreaming.

"You almost lost your story. It was flying away on the beach when I pulled the sailboat up to the pier. I think I caught most of it." Gabe's rogue smile caught her off guard. "Here you go."

Rory stared for a moment at the stack of papers and suddenly it dawned on her that he was holding words she'd written. "Thanks for gathering up the pieces of my manuscript." Her cheeks heated. Gabe was here. Had he read her story? Could he guess that this was a romance inspired by him?

"Don't worry I only read one page." How could he read her thoughts so easily?

"It's a romance. You probably wouldn't like it." Rory wasn't sure what books he read, but she was convinced romance wasn't one of them.

Quickly she grabbed the stack of papers. The love story she had written was inspired by Gabe and seemed much too private for him to read.

"*Au contraire.* I really like your writing. Although I am curious to read the rest of that last unfinished scene." Gabe winked at her, his blue eyes mischievous.

She swatted him with the manuscript in her hand knowing he was teasing.

An easygoing chuckle escaped his lips.

Flustered, she shoved the papers back in her tote bag thinking of the scene he was talking about. It was the scene where her heroine Adrianna had dropped the pepper shaker to the floor. The hero Jared had bent down to help her and they had almost kissed.

She had played a similar scene in her head about Gabe... many times.

Rory looked away for a moment trying to collect her thoughts fairly certain her cheeks couldn't get any warmer. She turned to peer up at Gabe only to see him reach his hand towards her.

Hesitantly she put her hand in his. Gabe pulled her close to him. She peered up at him, her knees going weak at the warm appreciation lingering in his large blue eyes.

Rattled, she stepped back and out of his arms. Her emotions were in conflict and uncertainty warred with desire. All of a sudden if felt like she had stepped into new territory.

"Want to go sailing with me?"

Maybe Gabe had sensed her unease? Asking her to go sailing was a request inside her comfort-zone. She replied easily.

"Now?" Rory looked out towards the end of the pier to see Gabe's beautiful large state-of-the-art sport sailboat floating near the end of the pier.

"It's a sunny day and the wind is just right. There's no time like the present." Gabe's handsome face held a hint of challenge.

A challenge she accepted. "Sure. I just need to call Aunt Florrie." Rory touched the number on her two-way walkie-talkie. She explained to her Aunt that Gabe was taking her on his sailboat. Rory told her she'd be careful and would be back in a couple of hours.

Rory slipped her two-way radio back in the pocket of her jean shorts.

"They're okay with that?"

"My aunts are more than okay with that. I'm pretty sure you can do no wrong in their eyes." Her lips turned up into a half-smile as she realized how true that was.

"Well, that's good to know. I hope that their niece feels the same." Gabe turned to look at her his rogue smile firmly in place as they walked along the pier.

Rory giggled. "Well, I know you a little better than my

Aunts and you can do plenty wrong. But, you're lucky because I still think you're fun." She gave him a friendly shove.

Without warning Gabe grabbed her waist and held onto her as he dangled her arms and legs over the water. "I can do plenty wrong?"

"Okay okay, I give." Rory laughed as she dangled there.

"And?" Gabe was waiting for his compliment. This was something he'd required of her ever since she was young. If she didn't agree he'd dangle her over the side of the pier once again.

"And you can do no wrong." Suddenly he turned her so she faced him.

As Rory slid down against his hard body warm tingles of awareness skittered across her skin everywhere her body touched his. As soon as her feet were planted firmly on the wooden dock she quickly stepped back.

Her senses were on overload after being so close to Gabe.

"I'm happy you know when to give up." He slowly removed his hands from her waist a big grin on his face.

Rory swatted him and hurried toward the sailboat. "Maybe I haven't completely given up. It's possible I'm strategizing when to make my next move. It might be when you least expect it."

He laughed out loud as he followed her. "That's what I love about you Rory. You're a woman who doesn't give up and is always finding a way to make her next move."

That's what he loved about her? She wanted to hug those words close to heart but she knew better. Now he was acting like the big brother he'd always been to her and his words were spoken casually in a moment of fun.

She shook it off and grinned at him hurrying to the end of the pier where his sailboat was anchored.

Gabe moved quickly to catch up and held out his hand to help her step into the boat. Her hand trembled slightly as she touched his. He pulled her close to his side with one hand and slipped the other around her waist to keep her steady.

Her body still tingled from his touch. It seemed his hand lingered at her waist longer than necessary. Rory forced herself to calm her emotions.

"Thanks. I think I've got it." As soon as Gabe pulled his hand away cool air settled at her waist. Rory hurried back to make room for Gabe as he stepped onto the deck of the boat and untied the rope from it's mooring.

"The wind has picked up. Sailing should be good today." Rory knew she was starting to babble. She did that when she was nervous. It had been so long since she'd been out sailing with Gabe. She stepped toward the center of the boat and stopped as the breeze caressed her face.

"You like this?"

"Oh Gabe this is wonderful. I've missed this." Rory sat on the long bench in the middle of the sailboat and closed her eyes letting the wind blow over her face.

Unmoving she enjoyed the breeze for a few minutes before she stood and walked over to the helm. "There's something peaceful about being on the water letting the wind blow across your cheeks."

"True. But I find you get a better feel for it when you're at the helm. It's been a few years since you've sailed. Do you remember how it's done?" An eyebrow quirked up as Gabe threw out the challenge.

He motioned for her to step in front of him and take control of the wheel.

"You'll need to re-fresh my memory." Rory was excited to handle the large boat. Gabe had practically grown up sailing and even though they'd done this before, she really needed a reminder for almost everything she needed to know.

She stood behind the helm with one hand tentatively on the wheel.

"Use both hands so you have a steady grip. I'll show you." Gabe stepped close behind her and placed his hands on hers.

Warm tingles spread from her hands up her arms at his touch. His chest rubbed against her back as he showed her how to steer the tiller to stay on course.

Muscled arms brushed against hers on both sides and she felt snuggled in a safe cocoon.

"So there's a few boating rules to remember. When two sailboats are approaching each other and the wind is on the same side of each boat, the boat that is windward - in the direction of the wind - must give the right of way to the vessel that is leeward. Another important guideline to remember is that if you get too close to another boat, whichever boat has the other boat on its starboard side - right hand side - must yield the right of way." Gabe's instructions were helpful and she only hoped she'd remember everything he taught her.

"Ah yes it's coming back to me. I feel like such a newbie." Rory gripped the wheel tighter and steered the boat away from a boat they passed on their starboard side.

"You always were quick at figuring things out."

"Well I have a fairly good teacher." Rory turned to look at him a wide grin on her face.

Gabe's face was close to hers and a whisper of his warm breath caressed her cheek as he spoke.

He was so close she could easily lean back into his arms. Scents of sand and sea rose off his skin and Rory inhaled deeply.

Lifting up her eyes she was lost in the intensity of his gaze — two blue pools that reflected her own desire — pools she could drown in. Those two blue orbs lowered from her eyes to hover over her lips. He started to lean down. Butterflies began to form in her belly as she anticipated her first kiss with the same man she'd been dreaming about for years.

Without warning a seagull screeched loudly overhead startling them both.

Abruptly they stepped back from each other.

Rory glanced at him an uncertain smile on her face before quickly turning to look forward.

With her gaze straight ahead she started babbling again. "Sailing is so wonderful. It's a place to breathe and feel safe." Rubbing her arms she let out a long sigh.

Don't dwell on that almost kiss. And don't show your disappointment to Gabe. Just let it go.

Rory swallowed quickly and looked over the quiet waters that surrounded them letting a rare moment of calm wash over her. They had slowed down a little and the waterway ahead was clear of boats for the moment.

Turning to look back at Gabe she noticed his brows puckered in worry.

"Why the serious face?"

"It's just a little disconcerting that one of your biggest concerns is for the safety of your aunts and yourself. I just worry about you that's all."

His words brought a smile to her face. She couldn't help but appreciate the fact that Gabe Stevenson — a man as well known as he was with thousands of other concerns — was worried about her.

Before she could speak he went on. "But just so you know, I did hire some workers to put hidden cameras around the cottage and around Grand's Hunting Lodge. And I'm doing more digging into who is behind the fire and who wants to ruin all your hard work."

"Thanks Gabe for doing that. I have to admit my worry is for my aunts." Rory bit her lip wondering how much to tell him. "There's just been some weird stuff happening on the Island for the past couple of years."

Gabe reached up and ran his finger along her forehead to smooth out the furrow between her eyebrows. A trail of warmth tingled her skin. "Your aunts told me. They also said that when you were a child someone sent a threatening note that something bad would happen to you when you got older."

"Yes." She nervously tucked a tendril of hair behind one ear. "Well, who knows what will happen. My aunts tend to worry too much about me. Besides, I still have two weeks before I turn twenty-one." Rory expelled a nervous laugh.

She couldn't help but shiver at the reminder. Who hated her that much that they wanted to hurt her?

"I think it's prudent to do what we can to keep you safe."

She nodded not trusting herself to speak.

"I want to help protect you Rory. I think I've come up with a way to do that." Gabe ran a hand through his hair, his bright blue eyes honing in on hers.

"Sounds good. What do you have in mind?"

His solemn expression made her wonder what he was thinking. She tensed, her hands suddenly sweating from nervousness.

"If you're by my side I can protect you." Gabe expelled a long breath, his gaze steady and focused on hers. "I'm asking you to marry me."

Rory's mouth dropped suddenly at his words. Her heart accelerated with excitement for a moment before she came down to earth.

He wasn't asking to marry her because he loved her. He was marrying her to protect her.

It was kind of Gabe, but she didn't want to marry for protection. She wanted to marry for love.

Now it seemed her dream that at one time had flared like a bright flame was suddenly burned to ashes.

CHAPTER FIVE

abe

As soon as the question left Gabe's lips an unexplainable longing filled him that he wished he could marry Rory for real.

He couldn't do that of course no matter how much he might want to. She was the girl he had hung out with most summers since she was six years old. He was like the older brother she never had.

Of course it made sense that he would protect her. Gabe would protect her like a brother. Not like a man in love.

The only thing this marriage would be — all it could be — was a necessary step to help them both get what they wanted.

Gabe looked over at Rory the corners of his lips turning up as her jaw dropped in surprise.

A mixture of emotions flitted across her face with all the force of a rising storm. For a moment he thought she would accept his proposal but all of a sudden her eyes narrowed as she turned to him.

"Please tell me you're not asking me to marry you because you feel sorry for me?" Rory crossed her arms and he could hear her toe tapping on the wood deck of his sailboat.

"No I don't feel sorry for you. I want to protect you." He could tell she softened a little at his words. "If it makes you feel better you would also be helping me too."

Rory shook her head and chuckled. "How in the world would marrying me help you out?"

"Because of the stipulation Grand put in his will." Gabe went on to tell her that he needed to be married by his twenty-seventh birthday to receive his inheritance.

"That's only a few weeks from now."

"I know." He waited a moment as she digested the news. She uncrossed her arms and turned to look at the water for a moment.

He hoped she would be open to listen to his thoughts on the matter. "It's sudden I know. But hear me out Rory. I was thinking this wouldn't be a real marriage. We could agree to make this a marriage-of-convenience for one year. You would get one million dollars and I would promise to do everything I could to see you and your aunts protected. Then at the end of one year we would part as friends."

The frown on Rory's forehead didn't bode well for her response to his proposal.

"A marriage-of-convenience. I didn't think people did that sort of thing anymore."

"Most people don't except it seems to be a thing in my family. Even my mom and dad's marriage started out as a marriage-of-convenience."

"Really?" Rory shook her head and look of surprise flooded her face. Gabe could almost see the wheels turning in Rory's mind.

"Yes. In fact to hear my mom tell it, at the beginning of their marriage my parents didn't get along. Yet they grew to love each other." Gabe remembered those early childhood years and how his dad and mom were always kissing each other. He was reminded of his two older brothers and the fact that they also were putty in their wives hands.

"That's great that it worked out so well for them." Her hands had a slight tremor in them as she reached for her jacket.

Gabe helped place it around her shoulders. She peered up at him, eyes flitting back and forth with uncertainty. "I'm not sure. I need a little time to think about your proposal okay?"

He slowed the sailboat so that it floated beside the long pier that stretched out from Walker's Island.

Gabe nodded. He leaned down to kiss her cheek. "Okay. I'll get back to you in a couple of days. I'll check in with you before I go to my mom's birthday party. You can give me your answer then."

He threw the rope around the wood pillar they used to tether the sailboat.

"All right. I'll see you later then." Her cheeks were flushed red. Rory nodded quickly before she hurried off the boat and toward home.

As Rory bolted away from him, a sudden unexplainable loss filled his senses.

Gabe realized he missed her already. He looked forward to the next time he saw her. He only hoped Rory would say yes to his marriage proposal.

If he were to be her husband Gabe felt like that would give him greater liberty to do everything he needed to so Rory was protected and safe.

CONFUSION FILLED her and thoughts swirled around in her head at Gabe's sudden marriage proposal.

He had been the man she'd dreamed about marrying for so long she surprised herself when she didn't say yes on the spot. But her dream had not been to get married because of a marriage-of-convenience agreement.

She wanted a man to choose her because he loved her.

Rory released a long sigh of frustration.

Why did her life seem so topsy-turvy lately? Why did the things that she wanted seem to come to her in different ways than she expected?

Looking up and past the tops of the tall poplar trees she said a quick prayer. She needed all the help she could get to figure out what to do next.

Turmoil churned in her belly at Gabe's unconventional request.

What she really needed was to talk to Raz. Through

the years she'd often talked to her friend when she needed advice. She needed to regain some perspective.

Razelle was a good friend and would listen and offer advice. Maybe she could set up a time when they could chat online.

As she neared the cottage she was surprised to see men working around their yard. They were setting up lights and rounded cameras onto steel poles that they'd placed around the perimeter of the yard. These must be the men that Gabe had hired.

Looking at their cottage and the rest of their backyard she imagined what it must look like to a visitor. Blackened grass and ruined outbuildings made it look like their house and yard had been in a war zone.

Gabe hired these men to add security cameras. I shouldn't dwell on the bad. Instead, I will focus on the good. There are a lot of reasons to be grateful.

For the first time someone else was helping to look out for them and it felt really good. She hadn't realized what a weight she carried with her fears for her aunts safety.

Next time she saw Gabe she would thank him again. Quickly she realized he wouldn't only want her thanks, but her answer.

For the first time she wondered if a marriage-in-name-only might be a good idea.

Gabe was continually doing things to help protect them all. By marrying him, it would solve her biggest concern for her aunts' safety. Even if Gabe didn't love her they would have his protection for one year and maybe by that time they would discover who was behind all the problems on the Island.

She was still pondering that when her dogs ran up to her each vying for her attention. They licked her hands and she patted their heads.

Hurrying into the house she spotted Aunt Florrie standing at the kitchen island mixing a batch of cookie batter.

Rory reached a finger in the bowl nibbling on the sweet batter. "Yum."

Grinning, Aunt Florrie lightly smacked her hand with the spatula when she tried to reach for more. "Don't spoil your supper."

"Please just one more taste?"

"All right. I never could say no to your wheedling ways." Her aunt eyed her. "Did you enjoy sailing with Gabe?" The twinkle in her eye made Rory want to play it down. Her three aunts had always had such great hopes for her and Gabe Stevenson.

She didn't want to get their hopes up.

"It was okay." Rory shrugged and saw the disappointment on Aunt Florrie's face. "We might go again soon. I need to re-learn how to sail." Her aunt's face brightened a little when she heard that. Rory reached her finger into the mixing bowl once more and licked the batter off her fingers.

"Thanks. You're the best." She kissed her aunt's cheek and hurried up the stairs to her room.

Quickly she changed into her old jeans and sweatshirt and sent a quick message to Raz. There was no response so Rory sent another message to ask if they could talk this evening.

Since Rory didn't know when her friend would get

back to her, today was a good day to mix the little bit she had left from the hand-harvested seaweed. She just needed to go to the green house to see if she could salvage anything from the empty bottles she'd kept there.

She had noticed her aunts' rosacea and eczema was acting up again.

It was critical that she make a larger batch of the skin cream mixture. It was mostly for her aunts, but there was also the summer festival in Paradise Lake to think about. The festival was in three weeks, and there were quite a few people who were counting on her to bring the cleaners, moisturizers, toners, facial oils, serums, masks and other treatments she had formulated.

Since the fire had ruined everything she was desperate. Rory grabbed the bottles of essential oils she kept in her room and brought them downstairs to the laundry room. She would have to do her mixing here.

After gathering what she needed she hurried outside. A loud crack of thunder split the sky spurring her to make a beeline for the green house.

The building was all but destroyed since the fire, but Rory wanted to see if any of the bottles she had kept underneath the large steel galvanized bowl were salvageable.

Stepping carefully into the blackened walls of what used to be the green house, she walked across the hard dirt toward the other end where she had kept the bowl.

Slipping gloves onto her hands, she squatted and reached over to grab the edge of the bowl lifting it. She breathed a sigh of relief at the sight of the glass bottles. They where dirty but untouched by the fire.

Dragging the galvanized steel tub toward her one by one she put the glass jars inside. As she reached for the last jar she noticed a small piece of paper inside.

Pulling it out she turned it over and read.

Rory your twenty-first birthday is soon. We won't forget.

She sucked in a quick breath.

Her hands shook as she held the slip of paper and stared at the words. It was obvious this was the same person — or people — who had set the fire in the first place.

Who would do this? It seemed fairly clear that whoever wrote this was someone who knew her or at least knew when her birthday was.

Trembling she put the note in her pocket. She couldn't let her aunts see this. It would only make them worry more.

Standing on shaky legs she carried the tub of glass jars to the house.

Thunder cracked loudly and the rain storm poured down on her like a forewarning of things to come.

Rory hurried into the house through the kitchen door and set the tub down in the laundry room. After changing into dry clothes she went to work mixing the skin care formula.

At her best estimate this new mixture would last about two weeks. She desperately needed to find some place where she could get a whole lot of seaweed and other sea plants in big batches.

If she could find a solution to that problem she'd have enough to create a formula that would last for months. And she could bring boxes of bottled skin creams to the people in Paradise Lake who were asking for more.

Rory thought about how to solve this problem as she worked. After a few hours she finished her work.

She checked if Raz had messaged her.

Opening her computer she saw her friend's familiar script.

I'd love to chat.

"I'm here now. Thanks for taking a few minutes out of your day. I have to admit I'm a little frazzled today.

"What's up Rory?"

"Lately there has been some weird things happening."

"Oh? Like what?"

"Whoever destroyed our backyard also left a note. I found it today." Rory went on to describe the threatening words.

"Rory you have to let the police know."

"I will. But first I want to show the note to Gabe because he hired a Private Investigator to search for clues as to how the fire started. Maybe the PI will be able to help with this."

"Okay. That's a good idea. This needs to be figured out before your birthday."

"Yes. But I feel like the PI will be the biggest help." Rory hesitated for a moment. *"Also I need your advice."*

"Sure. What's up?"

"Gabe took me sailing today. He shocked me when he asked me to marry him." Rory explained Walker Stevenson's will and about Gabe's request for a marriage-in-name-only.

"He what? That's sudden."

"It is. I'm still in shock."

"I think you should do it."

"Why do you think so?"

"Rory you've been in love with Gabe Stevenson over half of your life. He asked you to marry him and you said no?"

"I said I'd think about it. Gabe said he needed an answer in two days."

"You should marry him. You would finally be married to the man you've dreamed of for so long."

"Yes but will I be the only one in love? I wanted to marry a man who loved me too." Rory wanted that love and sense of belonging so badly she could taste it.

"I think he's half in love with you already but doesn't know it. He has promised to protect you and he's giving you money too? I wouldn't be surprised if he'll find a way to help you figure out a solution to get the sea plants you need."

"I suppose. Maybe I just need to think of this marriage-of-convenience the same way Gabe does. As a practical solution to get what we both need. If it will help my aunts then I will do this. Besides it's only for one year."

"There you go. And just for the record my friend, I think you're going to discover that you love being married to Gabe."

"Hmm, maybe that's what I'm afraid of." Rory texted. In all honesty it was one of her biggest fears to love a man who didn't love her back. She still remembered being five and six years old. Her father disappeared for weeks on end and her mom had been desperately lonely.

Maybe her memories weren't as clear as to what actually happened but that was the impression that lingered with her from when she was a little girl. Now those same memories caused her to think that any man she married might not love her and want to be with her as much as she needed him to.

"No fear Rory. Just watch and see what happens. It won't be long before he realizes he's in love with you."

"Not going to happen but I appreciate the sentiment." Aunt Merrie opened her bedroom door to tell her it was time for dinner. *"Got to go. Chat later?"*

"Of course!"

Rory closed her laptop and sat for a minute thinking of her chat with Raz. Her friend seemed fairly confident that Gabe would marry her and then fall in love with her.

She shook her head certain that wouldn't happen.

No, a marriage-of-convenience with Gabe would satisfy her if he saw to it that her aunts were protected.

Rory desperately tried to convince herself of this but failed.

She wanted so much more.

Nerves fluttered all up her legs and arms as Rory approached Walker Stevenson's Hunting Lodge.

Morning dew clung to her shoes from last night's rain as she trudged through the grass. It was a good mile walk from the cottage up the small hill to the large house that Walker Stevenson had built.

Gabe had planned to talk to her in a couple days, but she couldn't wait.

Since finding that alarming note yesterday anxiety coiled like a tight knot in her belly. She had hardly slept last night because of it and knew she couldn't go another day without talking to Gabe.

Approaching the Lodge, she spied the same workers who had been at the cottage the last couple of days. They were setting up steel poles to hold the hidden cameras all around the perimeter.

She walked around the building until she saw Gabe. He was talking with an older man who had on a hardhat and tool belt.

Curious, she walked closer to Gabe waiting in the shadows until he finished his conversation.

It wasn't long before Gabe spotted her.

His gaze ran up and down the length of her and settled on her face. Rory hoped his wide grin and the hint of appreciation that glimmered in his blue eyes meant he wouldn't mind her interrupting his day.

She noticed the old pair of jeans he wore and the Seahawks t-shirt that looked like it had seen better days. It annoyed her that he always looked good even wearing ratty clothes.

He walked toward her with his rogue smile firmly in place. "This is a nice surprise. I didn't expect to see you until tomorrow."

"Yeah well, I didn't expect it either. But it's important that I talk to you today." Rory looked at the dozens of workers all around them before peering up at Gabe. "Looks like you're busy."

"Just making some plans to renovate this place as well as sorting out ideas for the resort on the other side of the Island."

"A resort. Wow, that's a big project." Rory tried to imagine it in her mind.

"Yes it is. That's why I've been asking Bob my general contractor for his ideas on where we should start with such a big project." Gabe nodded and grinned at the man with whom he'd just finished talking. He looked at Rory a new glow in his eyes.

"I can tell you're excited."

"I guess I am. It's something that's been in the back of my mind for a year or two now."

Rory tried to ignore the sudden wave of apprehension that flooded her to hear Gabe talk about adding a resort to their Island. It was her home and she worried about being invaded by tourists.

Gabe folded his arms across his chest. "I know that look. Don't worry I intend to keep half of the Island private. It's only the southern half of Walker's Island that I'm thinking of making into a resort area."

"It's annoying how you do that you know." Rory shifted on her feet a little intimidated that her very thoughts seemed to be an open book to Gabe Stevenson.

"What? Read your mind?" He chuckled. "We spent a lot of summers together Rory. I know you better than you think."

Belatedly she realized just how true his words were. She wasn't sure why that made her uncomfortable. Maybe it was the fact that Gabe might know some of her secrets. It made her feel like running for cover.

The loud banging of a hammer in the background interrupted their conversation.

Not wanting to compete with the noise Rory leaned over and spoke in Gabe's ear. "Could we go talk somewhere private?"

"Want to get me alone already?" Gabe grinned as she grimaced and put her hands on her hips. He pointed in the direction of Grand's old Hunting Lodge.

Rory hurried beside him heat rising from her neck to her cheeks at his teasing. Gabe opened the door and Rory spoke. "I have something serious I want to discuss with you."

He closed the large rustic wood front door behind them and leaning up against it he spoke, his tone contrite. "I'm sorry Rory. I don't mean to get you riled. You're just so easy to tease." He held his hand out for her to walk ahead of him up the stairs and into the large great room.

She nodded and gave him a half smile as her acceptance of his apology and walked into the warmth of the great room. "I've always loved this room."

"I know me too. I can't bring myself to change anything about it. Too many memories I suppose."

Gabe's expression turned nostalgic as if remembering.

Rory had some pretty great memories of her own. "Your great-grandfather would invite my three aunts and I over when he was on the Island. I still remember Walker Stevenson sitting in that easy chair over there by the fireplace smoking his pipe or whittling on whatever new wooden toy he was making at the time. Funny, but I can still smell the scent of his pipe in this room."

Rory looked over at Gabe surprised to see the moisture in his eyes. "Me too." He said in a hushed whisper. The somber moment seemed appropriate for both of them.

Gabe walked over to the fireplace and added a log to the crackling fire. "Sit down and relax Rory. You look a little tense."

Rory grabbed a large cushion and placed it farther

away from the fireplace. Fire still filled her with fear and she preferred not to be too close. "Thanks."

As she watched the flames get higher her mind filled with all that she needed to tell Gabe.

"Tell me what's got you so worked up." Gabe's warm breath whispered in her ear. Rory turned not realizing he sat nearby. He handed her a glass of orange juice. She took a sip and reached into her pocket handing him the note.

"What's this?" Gabe turned it over and he read the jagged words. She watched as Gabe's face switched from serene to angry in a moment. "Who wrote this? It sounds like they are threatening you."

"I don't know. But I wanted you to see it. I thought maybe you could show it to that Private Investigator you hired." She couldn't help it that Gabe's protective attitude made her feel good inside.

"Don't worry I will show it to him. Where did you find it?"

Rory explained about looking for more bottles in their small burned out green house.

"Seems like whoever is doing this has been watching you for awhile now. They know where you keep things that are important to you."

A chill ran up her spine at Gabe's words.

She had avoided saying that out loud. Now that it was out there, it felt more real. Someone really was stalking her and trying to hurt her. She stared at the flames, fear tightening its grip on her once again.

"Do you know what they mean when they say they won't forget?" Gabe's soft voice barely reached her so deep was her fear. With gentle fingers under her chin he turned her head and looked deep into her eyes.

A single tear ran down her cheek as she slowly shook her head.

"It'll be okay Rory. Come here." He pulled her into his arms and she cried softly onto his wide shoulders. All the pent-up tension began to drain from her as she wept softly. He drew her closer until she was sitting on his lap and he kissed the top of her head. "I'll see to it that you'll be safe. Don't worry."

"I know you will." Rory pulled back a little and wiped her eyes. "Sorry I didn't mean to get all weepy on you."

"It's okay." His beautiful blue eyes were filled with warmth as he stared at her.

"There's one more thing I want to tell you." Rory hesitated and he waited patiently for her to go on. She worked up the courage to tell Gabe her decision. "I've thought about your offer and I accept with one condition."

The corners of his mouth turned up. "What's that?"

"All I ask is that my aunts don't find out that this a marriage-in-name-only." Rory watched until finally Gabe nodded.

"I agree. And the same thing holds true for my family. My mom and grandparents need to believe we married for love. So we're agreed?"

"Yes." Suddenly she smiled as a memory lingered in the back of her mind. "Besides you did promise a frightened six old that when she was older you would marry her and keep her safe."

She grinned at the memory of the wide-eyed boy back then who had looked so uncertain as seeing this new girl in tears. She had cried in fear and misery at the recent loss of her parents.

Being suddenly thrust onto this Island with three Aunts she didn't know very well — her mom's sisters — had made her feel insecure. It had all been very new and overwhelming.

Rory had been so fearful but Gabe had spent time with her and shown her things on the Island, which helped to make this her home. But at the same time he'd also promised to marry her if she was still scared when she grew up.

Gabe's expression shifted, his blue eyes gleaming as he stared into hers. "So I did."

All of a sudden the room sparked with the electricity of their attraction.

His hand brushed against her arm and moved up to tuck a loose strand of hair behind her ear. "I did make that promise. Now I intend to keep it."

A sizzling trail of heat burned her skin wherever he touched her.

Rory grew nervous as his gaze moved down to her lips. She suddenly became very aware of the fact that she was still sitting on his lap.

Scurrying over to her cushion she searched for anything that would divert his attention from her. With shaky hands she reached for her glass of orange juice and took a sip.

She started babbling again. "I'm glad we got that settled."

"Not quite. We need to set a date. I think we should get married next week." Gabe sounded very confident in his decision.

Rory thought of her aunts uncertain of their response. "I'm not sure how I'll be able to explain our quick wedding to my aunts."

"We'll tell both our families that we fell in love and didn't want to wait."

Rory sent Gabe a nervous smile and nodded.

She hoped they would both be very good at acting like a couple in love.

For Rory's part in this fake marriage she was very much afraid she wouldn't be acting.

She was very much afraid she was falling in love.

CHAPTER SIX

ory

THE RED-ORANGE GLOW of the sun was just beginning to touch the edge of the river behind them as Rory walked toward Gabe.

She wore her grandmother's wedding dress — an Audrey Hepburn style cocktail length 1950s wedding dress so similar to the one the actress wore in the movie *Funny Face.*

It had been her grandmother's dress when she was married. Aunt Merrie had tucked it safely away all these years but brought it out for her niece to wear for her wedding day.

His bride looked beautiful.

Ever since the summer Rory turned sixteen he'd

appreciated how attractive she was but today she looked stunning.

Shifting his feet he resisted the urge to loosen his tie.

He was still in shock that he was actually doing this. He was actually marrying Rory Shepard. If Winny O heard about this she would be pleased he took her advice and married his childhood friend.

Sitting in the front row were the smiling faces of his Mom and Grandmom and his two brothers and their wives making this all too real. His younger brothers Zach and Luke sat beside their mom.

Rory had agreed with him that a small wedding with only family and a few friends would be best.

As his bride glided closer looking as beautiful and pure as an untouched flower, Gabe wished suddenly that this wedding could be more than a marriage-of-convenience. Rory deserved better.

She deserved a man who would love her and commit to her for a lifetime.

Where did all these thoughts come from? Gabe shoved them back down before they had a chance to resurface.

No, they needed to stick to the plan. It had been his experience that women schemed to get what they wanted once they got a taste of his money and fame.

He didn't really believe Rory was like that but given time who knew what might happen?

Yet the warm look in her eyes as she looked up at Gabe's Granddad and then turned to her groom a shy smile hovering over her lips, mocked his cynical thoughts.

Now she stood in front of him like the loveliest of angels. His angel.

She was a rare woman.

He would need to watch that he didn't go beyond the boundaries they'd set up for this fake marriage.

Their relationship could only be based on friendship, not love.

He promised himself that he would make this year of marriage worth her while. He'd protect Rory and her aunts and do whatever he could to help with what she cared about most.

As he held his arm out she lightly put her hand on top of his and they turned to face each other.

Gabe hardly heard a word the pastor said as his gaze was glued to his bride.

His skin tingled with the light touch of her hand in his. Violet blue eyes shimmered like diamonds and he was drawn to his bride like a sailor longed for the sea.

He didn't know how long he stood there gazing into her eyes, but all of a sudden the pastor's words interrupted his churning thoughts.

"Gabriel Stevenson do you take Aurora Shepard to be your wedded wife?"

His voice cracked. "I do."

Rory's soft whisper repeated the words.

"You may kiss your bride."

In spite of his recent vow to keep a respectable distance from his fake wife Gabe found himself anticipating his first taste of her sweet lips.

He swept the shimmering veil away from her face and stepping close slipped one hand around her waist. He pulled his bride into his embrace and with his other hand caressed her jawline.

With slow movements he leaned down and gently pressed his lips to hers.

Gabe urged her closer wanting more.

His bride tasted like strawberry and cream. His bride made him think of warm summers and Island breezes. His bride reminded him of what it might feel like to love a woman with all his heart.

Abruptly he stepped back shocked at the raw emotions running through him.

Wide-eyed he stared at Rory his heart racing with the electricity of their kiss.

৯৯

RORY DIDN'T WANT Gabe's kiss to end.

Enfolded in her new husband's arms she felt the safest she'd ever been.

Not just safe but peaceful. And beyond that she felt loved.

Now that she'd said I do he was her husband and she wanted to go on kissing him forever. Her breath stilled as Gabe's mouth captured hers fully. Nipping and pulling his mouth caressed hers.

His warm lips molded against hers until she didn't know where his ended and hers began.

Her heart shuddered away in her ears like a loose wheel.

It was as if he had branded her, making her his.

Her legs melted and she tightened her grip on his arms.

She would gladly have kissed Gabe for much longer but suddenly he stepped away from her.

Gabe blue eyes darkened glued to hers like he'd never seen her before.

She understood the feeling.

Only she could tell he wasn't pleased that their kiss had affected him.

Her own thoughts barged in setting up a barricade against her hopes and dreams.

Remember Rory you agreed to be Gabe's wife-in-name-only. Don't you dare let your heart get involved or you'll end up with it broken into tiny pieces. Besides you can tell your new husband is not happy about that kiss. So just smile and pretend for today. You can do this.

Gabe's arm went around her waist and they both turned to look at their family and friends as the pastor announced them as husband and wife.

The wedding guests' clapped loudly and she turned toward them a smile pasted on her lips.

Soon their family and friends encircled them with well wishes.

"Oh Rory you look dazzling in your Grandmother's wedding dress." Aunt Merrie kissed her cheek moisture in her grey eyes. "I thought I'd never want to see that dress again since I was left at the altar over thirty years ago. But seeing you wearing it today has convinced me to change my mind."

Rory squeezed her aunt a little tighter feeling an inexplicable sadness at her heartache.

"It's all right my dear. I've had years to heal." Aunt Merrie whispered in her ear before she stepped back. She looked at her two sisters who were close behind her. "If your blessed mama and grandmother were here, they would agree you look so beautiful."

"I agree." Aunt Fawn stepped closer to Rory, her cane wobbling slightly.

Rory wrapped her arms around her. "Thanks for being here today, Aunt Fawn. I know you must be in a lot of pain with all the walking you've done."

"Always so thoughtful. Thank you Rory for thinking of me, but you know I wouldn't miss your wedding day for the world."

Aunt Florrie stood behind Aunt Fawn helping to hold her steady. "I agree. You are so beautiful." She gave her a quick hug before she continued, "But I think it's time we helped your Aunt Fawn to the tables so she can sit down."

Rory nodded. "Yes of course." She was already missing her three aunts as they walked away.

It wasn't long before Rory was engulfed in massive hugs from Gabe's two single brothers. "Happy you're part of our family now, sis. I just want to give you a heads up. Don't let my big brother railroad you into anything." Luke winked at her and kissed her cheek.

Heat burned Rory's cheeks. She was sure her cheeks were red from all the attention. Not growing up with brothers put her at a distinct disadvantage. She didn't know what to do with all this brotherly attention.

"Don't listen to my little brother darling." Gabe leaned down and whispered his lips moving against her ear. "Besides I wouldn't railroad you into doing something, I'd charm you instead. That would be much more appealing."

The warmth of Gabe's breath against her ear sent a

shiver up her spine. She liked it when he used endearments. Problem was she liked it a little too much.

Quickly she tamped down her longing for more from Gabe with the reminder that her fake husband was simply acting his part.

Turning to him she gave him her warmest smile. "I agree."

"Ugh, newlyweds." Rory giggled at Luke's exaggerated sigh before he walked away.

Before long Adam and Elle walked up to them offering their congratulations, as did Jack and Bella.

"Welcome to the Stevenson family Rory. I look forward to getting to know you. It's an adventure to be part of this family, but I wouldn't change it for anything." Elle hugged her. "We'll need to get to know each other. Maybe you can come riding with me at the ranch sometime."

"I would love that." Rory remembered hearing how Elle had nearly lost her father's ranch. Adam had bought the place and given her the deed. But, Elle had helped to save Adam and to help him get unstuck from a cycle of self-blame.

Bella was standing right behind Elle. Rory knew Bella better as they had worked at the Library together for a while before Bella married Jack. Now they would be family as well as friends — at least for a little while.

"Rory you are beautiful today. Welcome to the Stevenson family. I'm so happy that now you're my sister." Bella grabbed her in a big hug. Bella had always been a hugger and her tight embrace helped Rory feel so welcome.

Gabe's Granddad grabbed him in a quick embrace. "I hope you know we came home early from a nice sunny vacation for this. But never mind it was worth it."

"Hush William. Our grandchildren are going to think a vacation is more important than their wedding. Which certainly isn't true."

Gabe pulled his Grandmother into a soft hug a grin on his face. "You tell him Grandmom."

"Rory these two Stevenson men are rascals and more alike than they care to admit. It's up to us, their wives to help bring out their softer sides." Catherine Stevenson winked at Rory.

She grinned at the teasing between them. "I'll do my best."

"That's my girl. Welcome to the family my dear." Gabe's Grandmom and Grandad each wrapped her in a close embrace. Rory was overwhelmed by all the love shown to her.

"Rory, my newest daughter." Eliza Stevenson approached her with a shine of tears in her eyes. "All those summers we spent with Gabe's great-grandfather and the family here on the Island, and I never realized my son was falling in love with the girl-next-door. I'm so glad he did. Welcome to the family." Eliza's gentle embrace was Rory's undoing.

Swallowing back tears that threatened to choke her, Rory savored being encircled in her new mother-in-law's arms.

Memories came back of when she was a little girl and running into her Mom's arms whenever something important happened in her life. Now being in Eliza

Stevenson's arms, for the first time in a long time she felt the warm embrace of a mother's love and it was like coming home.

Her three aunts had raised her like their own daughter and she loved them so much but there was something quite special about being welcomed so warmly by her new husband's Mom.

"Thank you Mrs. Stevenson. I'm so honored to be part of your family." Rory wiped away a tear from her cheek and peered into the smiling face of her mother-in-law.

"I'd rather you called me Mom, Rory. Now we're family." Gabe's mom gazed into her face a moment longer. "You are beautiful inside and out. I can see why much my son loves you so much." Eliza leaned over to give her a light kiss on the cheek before she walked away.

Hesitantly, she turned to look up at Gabe. His Mom's words surprised her and she couldn't help but look at Gabe. Did he feel the same kind of guilt she did that they made his family believe they were in love?

Her husband settled his hand on the small of her back as they walked toward to where the tables were setup for their evening dinner.

The orange-red glow from the sunset lingered in the sky and twinkling lights outlined the large green space. Between the romantic setting and the warm look that glowed in her new husband's eyes for a moment it felt like she was a princess in a fairytale.

"Your Mom and Grandparents have been so wonderful. I feel like I'm part of your family."

"That's good because you are part of our family now Rory." Gabe wrapped an arm around her waist and leaned down to kiss her cheek. She glowed inside from his words and wished her marriage to Gabe was so much more than a legal document with a time-limit.

During her childhood when the Stevenson family had visited the Island, she had watched them from afar and longed to be part of such a loving close-knit family.

Today she had married into this wonderful family for real, but she still felt like she was standing with her nose pressed up against the window. She was still an outsider looking in.

Rory squared her shoulders as they neared the tables. She did her best to shake off the loneliness. *Courage Rory. You can get through this.*

Servers walked back and forth between tables and conversation buzzed around them.

They sat down and soon were served their meal.

Gabe showered her with attention and she grew frustrated with herself that his loving gestures affected her so deeply. They were supposed to remember their agreement.

His blue eyes held hers with a warm caress. She shivered at his attention and started to grow slightly irritated. How come Gabe didn't seem to be affected by the fact that they needed to act like a couple in love?

Rory sighed, reminding herself to relax and enjoy this day.

She smiled as Mr. And Mrs. Sterling stopped by and handed a piece of paper for Gabe to sign. Rory knew it was the official deed of ownership to Walker's Island. She was happy Gabe got what he wanted from this marriage-of-convenience. Why did it seem like their goals and desires came at such a high price?

"Ah young love. Thank you so much for the invitation. We must be getting home but we wanted to say congratulations to you both." Mrs. Sterling squeezed Rory's hand.

After the couple left a few other people stopped by to chat with them.

Another older couple approached them. "Gabe we just had to stop by to congratulate you and your wife and send you off with a little extra something." The large man neared her husband and slapped him on the shoulder. "This must be your beautiful wife."

Gabe put his arm around her shoulders and pulled her close to his side. "Cyrus and Anna I'd like to introduce you to Rory Stevenson, my bride."

She blinked at being called by the new last name, but recovered quickly. Rory could tell that this couple was important to her husband. "Pleased to meet you both. Thank you for joining us."

"Oh my dear, Gabriel is like a son to us. We've been waiting for this special day. We wouldn't have missed this for the world." The older woman wore a designer dress that was simple and beautiful. The older man was a large mountain man and his large hand engulfed hers.

"After you all get back stop by and tell us how you liked the place." Cyrus spoke to Gabe.

"I'll do that. Thank you Cyrus and Anna." The older couple walked away and Gabe picked up his glass and took a sip.

"They seem nice. What did they mean about stopping

by to tell them about the place? Where are we going?" Rory was more curious than ever.

Gabe winked at her. "You'll find out in due time. For now there are other more important things to focus on that are a lot more fun."

In the background the live band started playing a slow-moving waltz.

Gabe reached his hand out to hers. "Dance with me?"

Knowing this first dance as newlyweds was important she nodded and placed her hand in his. He led her to the large wood dance floor in the center of the green space. Spread out around them were tables with wedding guests and Rory could feel their eyes on them.

"It's difficult being the center of all this attention." Rory whispered as Gabe put his arm around her as they moved together in the rhythm of the waltz.

Gabe pulled her closer and she leaned her head against his shoulder. "You get used to it."

Rory sighed and spoke softly, "I don't know that I will get used to it. I'd much rather it was just you and me together like how it used to be." She sucked in a breath as she suddenly realized how that sounded. She began to apologize, "Sorry, I shouldn't have…"

Gabe put two fingers to her lips. "No, don't be sorry. I like that thought. Let's pretend its just you and me together just like it used to be, right at this moment." His blue eyes shimmered with a new awareness. His eyes searched hers gentle and warm.

"I'd like that." Waves of nervousness and anticipation skidded up her spine sending heat to her cheeks.

Gabe put both arms around her waist and pulled her close to him.

Blue eyes flickered in the evening light looking into her eyes with appreciation and a hint of something more.

Rory's belly flipped upwards as her husband lowered his head to hers. He kissed her forehead and the tip of her nose before he finally settled his warm lips on hers.

She wanted his kiss to go on forever, but also knew she couldn't do this not without it ending in heartache.

As the song slowed and the music faded, she pulled away from his close embrace.

Desperately she wanted this fake marriage to be the real thing. Desperately she wanted her husband to truly want her for who she was. Desperately she wanted to be totally loved by her husband.

As Gabe held his wife in his arms, he breathed in the scent of wildflowers that he had always reminded him of his Island girl.

Kissing her felt like coming home and it scared him.

He feared what being vulnerable would cost him.

If he truly began to open up his heart to his new wife would she spurn him or maybe use him in some way? He'd had his share of experiences with people who had wanted to use him before.

Memories from as far back as middle school all of sudden came back to haunt him. He didn't want to go through that again.

Without warning, Rory pulled herself out of his arms.

Disappointment and relief warred inside him.

He was disappointed because he admitted to himself that holding his lovely wife in his arms gave him pleasure. Relieved because having her so close and facing these new emotions had shaken him to the core.

"Thank you Gabe. That was magical." The country love-song that had been crooning in the background slowly faded away as he gazed into her violet blue eyes.

"I think that's my line." Gabe leaned over to whisper in her ear. He saw the corner of her lips turn up into a smile.

Just then his Granddad walked over to them interrupting their dance. "I believe this is my dance with my new Granddaughter."

"Hurry back, my love." He winked at Rory and saw her cheeks blossom into a beautiful pink color.

It was thoughtful of his Granddad to dance with his bride especially since Rory's own dad was no longer with them. He went in search of his Mom. He danced with her and each of Rory's three aunts in turn.

As he brought Rory's Aunt back to where his bride was seated suddenly Gabe was anxious to be alone with her.

Even though he realized this wasn't a real marriage he couldn't wait for Rory to see where he planned to take her.

Would Rory be pleasantly surprised?

He really hoped so because more than anything Gabe realized he was eager to please his new bride.

CHAPTER SEVEN

ory

A COOL DRY breeze blew hair across her face as she stepped down from the plane.

Gabe hadn't told her where they were flying. Last night all he'd told her was that she would find out tomorrow.

Surprising her, he'd whisked her away quickly from the wedding guests bringing her to his private plane.

She'd slept until Gabe had woken her late this morning. The comfort of the bed in the swaying jet had lulled her to sleep.

They had both changed into the familiar comfort of jeans and t-shirt. Her new husband had thought of everything it seemed. He'd even asked her aunts to fill her suitcase with clothes she'd need for a week.

Rory had been pleasantly surprised at his thought-fulness.

Gabe held her hand as they reached the landing.

Together they followed a friendly airport worker toward the terminal.

Rory's wide-eyed gaze took in the tiled roof and the Spanish styled architecture of the airport and nearby buildings. "Where are we? Surely you can tell me now that we've arrived."

"This is Puerto Madryn a port city in the Chubut Province of Patagonia, Argentina." She raised her eyebrows as they entered the building.

Around them she could hear different languages of Spanish, German, English and even a few people speaking Welsh. "What a wonderful surprise."

"I'm glad you think so." Gabe spoke quickly to one of the airport attendees and soon they were walking outside to where a driver waited for them.

After Gabe gave the street address he settled in the back seat beside Rory.

"I like this. But I never would've guessed you would choose an out-of-the-way place like Patagonia for our wedding trip. Care to tell me why we're here?" Never had she thought her new husband more of an enigma than today.

There was still so much to learn about Gabe Stevenson.

"For a few reasons." Gabe blue eyes stared at her for a moment before speaking. "I wanted to take you some-where fun and surprising."

"Looks like it is." She grinned as she saw a boat

heading out toward to sea. There were people on board holding their cameras ready. "What are they doing?"

"Whale watching. This area is known for its abundance of whales that show up from June to December. They give birth to their calves here during that time and teach them how to swim. I was told it's something most tourists like to see."

Rory eyes lit up. "I'd adore seeing the whales close-up."

"Then we'll plan to go."

"Thank you Gabe." She quirked her eyebrow at her husband. "And other reasons you chose to come here?"

"I hope you'll find this trip helpful."

"Helpful? I don't understand." Rory wondered what he had up his sleeve this time. Gabe certainly was full of surprises.

"Not far from this city are a few small Spanish and Welsh speaking villages. I did my homework and learned that this region has some of the best places to hand-harvest seaweed, kelp and marine algae."

"Really?" Rory put a hand to her mouth overcome that Gabe had gone to so much effort to see that she had what she needed to make her skin care products.

"Yes."

"So potentially I could find someone or a few people who would help me gather a big batch of sea plants I need to bring back home?"

"Yes." Gabe eyed her thoughtfully. "And something to consider is contracting out the work to a family who would supply you with all the sea plants you need to expand your organic skin care line of products."

Rory raised an eyebrow at his big plans. "You have

such lofty ideas. But, I suppose that's something to think about. I do keep getting more requests to make extra."

Rory shivered a little at Gabe's grand ideas. It hit her suddenly that there was a lot more to her new husband than she realized.

"I need to think some more about it. But thank you Gabe. It's so thoughtful of you to bring me here to see all this." Rory turned away for a moment and dabbed at tears trying to escape the corners of her eyes.

"You don't know how I've worried that I wouldn't have what I needed to formulate my skin creams. You are incredibly thoughtful."

"We're a team. That's why I wanted to help." Gabe reached over and placed his hand on top of hers. "I'm glad to do it. But I have to admit to a little selfishness on my part."

Curious she raised an eyebrow and waited. "I also wanted to stay at one of Cyrus Noble's resorts along the beach for my own research purposes as I plan the Walker Island resort."

"Research, right." The corners of her mouth turned up and she rolled her eyes at him.

Looking out the car window at the luxurious resort the driver pulled up to, she could only wish all research would be like this.

Rory's sucked in a breath at the sight.

The vast white sandy beach and ocean was beautiful. The resort was located on the beach and she could already hear the white sand and beach calling her name.

She giggled and looked back at him.

Gabe shrugged and grinned. "Who said research needs

to be dreary? This kind can only be fun." Her husband stepped out of the car and held out his hand to help her. "Come on. Let's go have some fun of our own."

The concierge took their bags and Gabe tucked her hand in his pulling her close to his side.

Her hand felt small in his but she liked how closely connected she felt to him. They were led to a room on the top floor with an incredible view of the city, beach and ocean.

It wasn't long before a maid knocked on their door.

"I'll be your personal butler and server this week." A beautiful girl with dark brown hair and large brown eyes met them at the door.

She looked to be about the same age as Rory. The maid seemed incredibly shy as she only looked up at them once. Her Spanish accent was noticeable as she spoke. "Let me hang up your clothes." She had just reached for the suitcases, when Rory interrupted.

"We appreciate your help. What is your name?"

"My name is Maria." Hesitantly she glanced upwards as her small hands gripped the bags tightly. "If you need anything just ask for me and I'll take care of it." She smiled bobbing her head a little before taking their bags to the bedrooms.

Rory turned to follow Gabe who walked over to the large picture window. "It's really nice to have someone take care of the details. This really is going to be a stress-free vacation."

Gabe pointed toward the ocean. "And a beautiful one."

Her gaze followed his and she gasped in awe at the beauty that greeted her. The beginnings of a red-orange glow of the sun dipped down touching its tip to meet the ocean. She stared out the window for a long time enjoying the varied bursts of color.

"Want to go for a walk on the beach before we find something to eat?"

"That would be nice."

Gabe reached for her hand and they hurried down to the first level of the resort.

"The air is a little cool." Rory shivered as they walked out of the building.

"The resort manager said we arrived at a great time as the weather is warmer than usual for this time of year. But here, slip this on." Gabe took off the hoodie he wore. "Hold your arms up."

"Wait, what about you?"

"I'll be okay. I don't feel the cold much." Gabe slid the hoodie over her arms and she poked her head through the top. He hesitated for a moment before he tugged the bottom of the hoodie.

A throbbing warmth began every place his hands touched her body as he shimmied the hoodie down to her waist.

Memories invaded her senses of the incredible kiss he'd given her on their wedding day.

Was that only yesterday?

Inhaling the scent of her husband - sandalwood mixed with the salty ocean breeze - caused childhood memories to once again pop up in her thoughts.

It reminded her of the many summers when she'd gone sailing or walked on the beach with Gabe. Those summers when she'd been a teenager and had such an unending crush on him.

She was pretty sure each of her aunts had noticed her feelings for Gabe. Heat rose in her cheeks still feeling embarrassed about the way she'd crushed on him back then.

"Walking on the beach at sunset reminds me of summer picnics and campfires on Walker's Island that lasted until late into the evening." Warmth flooded her as she thought about those days.

"Yeah that was fun. I especially remember when your aunts were busy telling Grand about some new thing they were doing and we would move away from the campfire to stargaze. We caught some great sights in the sky." Gabe commented and looked up at the dark night sky.

The sunset had since disappeared and it was dark except for the glittering lights of the city, some scattered campfires and the stars shining above.

"This far south makes it seem like the stars are not in their normal position." Rory stopped and looked up at the twinkling lights in the night sky.

"That's because for those of us who live in the north it seems like the constellations are all upside-down here in the southern hemisphere."

It made sense but it made it more difficult for Rory to find her favorite stars. "Where's the Milky Way?"

Gabe stepped behind her and held her hand. "Point your finger and I'll help you trace the Milky Way."

His strong arms wrapped around her while his warm breath tickled her ear. Her hand tingled where he held hers moving her hand to point at the different stars. "Can you see it?"

"Yes, I do. I guess it just confused me because it seems upside-down."

"Understandable. It took me awhile to figure it out too. The best part of stargazing this far south, is we get to see the nearest star to our Sun, *Alpha Centauri.* Not far from it is the smaller star, *Beta Centauri* and if you keep going higher you'll see the *Southern Cross."*

Once again Gabe took her hand and traced the stars to help her find them.

"Oh Gabe, it so mesmerizing that it takes your breath away." The twinkling of the stars lit up the night sky in varying shades of blue, white and yellow. Some were large, some were like tiny sparkling diamonds, but the backdrop created a beautiful canopy in the heavens above.

"I agree." She lowered her arms and her husband wrapped his muscled arms around her own. She realized he was the perfect height for her as his chin rested on top of her head.

Memories of early childhood came back to her suddenly.

"I still have a vivid memory of my Mom and Dad standing on their deck that was just outside their upstairs bedroom. They were looking up at the stars. I must have been five years old at the time." She swallowed back tears. "I remember them standing just like we are now. They always liked to stargaze together."

Her voice cracked as the night of her sixth birthday came back to her in vivid color. "That's where they were found after that horrible night of the fire."

She dabbed at her eyes with the sleeves of Gabe's hoodie desperate to hold back the torrent of tears. "The police told us my parents had been on the balcony stargazing and had forgotten about the candles they had left burning. That's how they died."

"I'm so sorry Rory." Gabe whispered his voice husky. He turned her around and with gentle hands pulled her into a close embrace.

His gentle words and tender touch were her undoing.

Sobbing she wept on his shoulder shaking from the loss of the two people whom she had loved most in the world.

Gabe rubbed his hands up and down her back murmuring words of comfort into her ear.

The trauma of that night came back at different times and each time a memory was triggered by something she'd seen or heard back then.

"You know what the really weird thing about that night was? My Mom didn't even like candles. I just don't understand why she had to light them that night. If she would've left well enough alone or if I would've checked on them before I went to bed that night my Mom and Dad would still be here with me." Rory choked out the real cause of her pain.

"That is strange." Gabe words came out slowly as if he was deep in thought. It was a full minute before he spoke again. "But you must know that it's not your fault that your parents died that night. You were only a child."

"I know the police told me and my aunts it was an accident, but it doesn't change the fact that they are gone and I was left alone without my parents." Rory pulled back and wiped her eyes with the sleeves of his hoodie once more.

"I'm here for you Rory whatever you need." Gabe's whispered words of support lifted her spirits.

Without thinking she stood on tiptoes, moving her hand up to cup his jawline and leaned forward to kiss his cheek. "Thank you Gabe. Your words mean so much to me."

His arms had slipped around her waist but as she settled back flat footed on firm ground his arms loosened and slipped away. A chill swept over her at the loss.

She didn't know what he was thinking. It was difficult to read his facial expression with the dark night around them.

"I'm sorry Gabe for blubbering all over you. I guess it really hit me as we looked at the stars tonight how much I miss them." Rory's voice shook.

Gabe's large hand wrapped around hers. "It's okay. I get it."

Rory realized she had made this night so much about her feelings without a thought for his. "I'm sorry Gabe of course you understand. I've selfishly only thought of my own loss. You also lost your Dad when you were young."

"Don't worry about it."

"No please Gabe I want to know. I've taken up all this time talking about me, but I really want to understand you better. For instance I know something we share is the loss of at least one of our parents. Will you tell me what happened?" Rory persisted.

For some reason she felt a need to really understand this defining moment of his life.

"Lets start walking back and I'll tell you what I remember." Rory walked close to his side as he began. "I was thirteen years old. My Mom worked part-time as a secretary and my Dad ran a business with his partner Simon Black."

Gabe rubbed his forehead before going on. "I remember it was just before summer holidays when school was ending and Dad would come home stressed everyday. Sometimes I would overhear him talking to Mom about how it seemed like his partner was telling their clients to take unnecessary risks with their finances."

He took a deep breath before he continued, "Simon had told him it was fine because he was convinced the risks wouldn't harm their clients and it would increase the income in their business. Dad would come home really upset sometimes. I could tell things were about to come to a showdown between my Dad and Simon."

Gabe looked off into the distance and Rory waited for him to continue. "Sure enough it happened. Only one week later I stopped by my Dad's office and heard a lot of yelling and arguing. I remember huddling in the corner chair in the front office unsure whether I should stay or go home. Dad's secretary had already gone home for the day and I was alone in the main office."

He rubbed the back of his neck and breathed in quickly. "I overheard what they were saying. It was the same old argument with Simon saying it's not going to hurt anyone, and my Dad convinced they needed to be honest in all their business dealings. Simon gave my Dad an ultimatum."

Gabe paused a moment. "He told Dad if he didn't agree with the way he did business he would take their biggest clients and leave the business. My Dad told him he couldn't do that because they signed a contract. To which Simon replied *you think I can't find loopholes around that? You'd best think about it Daniel. You know if those three biggest clients were gone that would leave you with great loss and no hope of recovery."*

Rory could feel the tension in Gabe's voice as he spoke. "What happened?"

"The next day when my Dad went to work he discovered the client files were missing and so was the money from the business account that he shared with his business partner. Simon must have panicked and ran." Gabe shook his head as he remembered. "Dad was devastated. He had a heart attack and died a few days later."

Rory slipped her hand in Gabe's with a gentle squeeze. "I'm so sorry."

Gabe squeezed her hand in response. His voice shook. "Thanks. It was especially tough for my Mom after that. My Dad was gone and all the money was gone. We really struggled to make ends meet. So my older brothers Adam and Jack took on full-time jobs and I took on a part-time job. I was young, but I knew how to work and get things done. I started a newspaper job and by the time I was a freshman, I was the local High School student reporter at our small town radio and TV station. We were able to pay the bills and pay the lawyer who eventually got Simon Black sent to jail."

"I'm glad your family's situation started getting better." Rory thought about Gabe's growing up years and realized she hadn't known all the difficulties that had gone on in his family. "Going through all that must have been so hard."

"Yes it was. At the time I felt so vulnerable and was going through so much anxiety from it all. I went through self-blame and wondered what I could have done differently to help my Dad." He paused for a moment. "I didn't want to put all those negative thoughts and worries on you."

They were near the lighted area of the resort and Rory could see his brows puckered together in worry.

"Gabe why would you blame yourself?"

"Because whenever I would see Dad's partner I would get this sickening feeling in the pit of my stomach. I knew something wasn't quite right about him but I never told my Dad. I guess I just assumed he knew. Maybe if I would have said something sooner my Dad could've stopped Simon from blackmailing him. And then he wouldn't have died." He choked on those last words and stopped. Closing his eyes for a brief moment Gabe swallowed and hesitated before he turned to face her.

Rory placed a gentle hand on his arm. "You can't know for sure what would've happened even if you said something. You can't continue to blame yourself Gabe."

"My head knows that but my heart still struggles with it. I think that's why I made up my mind not to allow myself to be in a vulnerable position like my Dad."

Rory digested his words for a moment before she spoke. "Is that why you began to write books and do trainings on self-development?"

"Yes. At first I started learning about how to improve myself but then I realized so many other people needed to learn how to grow themselves and how to safe-guard themselves against people who might want to take advantage of them." Passion was in Gabe's voice as he spoke.

Rory was sad at all the difficulties he'd experienced. "That's really great that you've dedicated so much of your life to helping others better themselves. It's terrible when people are treated poorly like your Dad. Has that happened to you?"

"Sadly, yes. I have been used quite a lot. Most of the time by women who want my money or my platform or something. It's never me they want. It's always something else." Gabe's mouth formed a firm line and he pulled his gaze away from her.

"That's horrible. I didn't realize that. Is that why you never married — I mean weren't married?" She sent her new husband a sheepish half-smile and the sun-bronzed skin around his eyes crinkled.

"Don't forget you're married now. To me." Gabe teased then turned serious once more and shifted his feet. "Yeah all the women I've dated so far haven't been interested in me as a person. I became really tired of it. Not long ago I dated a woman who had me twisted around her finger. I thought this relationship might be serious enough for marriage until I found out she had another guy on the side. Turns out she was interested in my money and the spotlight just like the others."

"Maybe someday you'll find a woman who doesn't care about the money or being in the spotlight and just loves you for who you are." Rory didn't know what made her say that. Inside she really wanted that person to be her. But Gabe was her childhood friend and she wanted only his happiness.

"I don't think that's going to happen." Gabe set his jaw in a firm line. He looked at the lights of the resort and back to her a mask hiding his emotions. "But I'm grateful you agreed to this short-term marriage Rory. You're a good friend."

Rory felt complimented and deflated all at the same time. She loved that he saw her as a good friend but his words *short-term marriage* weren't words she particularly wanted to hear right now.

But she didn't want Gabe to know the reminder stung.

She forced a smile. "Thanks Gabe."

"Anyway, let's agree to get out of this serious conversation and focus on having fun. That's what we're here for right?"

"I agree." Rory's smiled slipped a little and she yawned. "But I am feeling a little tired. Maybe we can save the fun for tomorrow?"

Gabe nodded almost too quickly.

They walked back to the Resort and into their shared suite of rooms, saying a quick goodnight. Rory retreated to her bedroom thinking for a long time about everything Gabe had told her.

She never realized all the details behind his father's sudden passing. It seemed the betrayal of his Dad's business partner had made Gabe fearful of being vulnerable. That along with the fact that he hadn't yet met a woman who liked Gabe for who he was.

That surprised her.

Her husband was a great guy even without all the

attachments of money and fame. Why couldn't people see that?

Maybe it was her job to help him discover that not all people were after something he had.

Maybe it was her job to help him discover that he didn't need to fear trusting the right person.

Maybe it was her job to help him discover that he was worthy of love simply for who he was.

CHAPTER EIGHT

abe

THE MORNING SUN was just beginning to rise in the clear blue sky as Gabe jogged back to the Resort.

As usual the run helped clear his head of troubling thoughts to gain a better perspective.

A better viewpoint was what he needed.

All night long he had tossed and turned. His thoughts were filled with his new wife.

Rory had a way of listening that made him want to tell her everything about his life. She had asked him some real personal questions last night.

His soul had been stripped bare and he didn't like it.

Talking about his how his Dad had been betrayed and

how the stress of that had caused his early death was a very touchy subject for him.

He still missed his Dad something fierce everyday of his life. The memory of how he had failed to tell his Dad what he sensed about Simon still haunted him to this day.

All these years of helping others with his self-development training still hadn't made up for the fact that deep down he felt like he'd failed his Dad when he needed him most.

It was such a vulnerable and painful place inside of him — it was the place where fear lived.

He had a fear of being taken advantage by someone who wanted to use him. Fear of letting down the people he loved. He had a fear of letting his guard down to allow people into his heart.

Rory had a glimpse into his heart last night and it scared him.

What shook him to the core was the affect she had on him.

Gabe was convinced that a marriage-in-name-only to Rory would be like all those summers they spent together as friends. He assumed they would have fun together and that would be it.

Yet, last night when they were stargazing together he felt closer to her than ever before. Listening to Rory share a story from her past made him long to do more than put his arms around her.

He wanted to kiss her with a passion that he was convinced would terrify her.

There was a moment last night when he could've touched his lips to hers but he had forced himself to be a gentleman. He had reminded himself that Rory was not only like a sister but she trusted him with a marriage-of-convenience.

But he'd wanted to kiss her… oh how he wanted to.

Now that he had his morning run, maybe now he'd be able to refocus.

He opened the door to their suite of rooms quietly so as not to wake her.

Stepping into the room he looked around and finally saw her sitting with her knees up on a large cushioned lounge chair that overlooked the swimming area.

His wife held a coffee cup in both hands with soft blond hair falling in waves across her shoulders.

The sleep tousled look did not help with his new resolve to treat Rory as a friend only.

So much for refocusing.

"Morning." He stepped inside and closed the door shrugging out of his hoodie before walking toward her.

"Morning Gabe. You're up so early. You had a morning jog huh?" He nodded and she continued, "I should've done that myself. My only excuse is that I was feeling lazy and so relaxed this morning."

"Good. A few lazy hours in the morning sounds good."

"I ordered room service. Maria should be here soon with our breakfast." Rory took another sip of the steamy drink and a layer of white foam formed above her pink lips.

"You have a white foam mustache." Gabe stared at her lips, thinking how much he would love to taste the white foam and remove it her lips.

His wife flicked her tongue across her top lip removing the foam.

Gabe stepped back and promptly pulled his thoughts away from wayward desires. "I'm going to shower quickly."

He hurried to his room and into the shower. As he stepped out of the hot mist he realized they needed to get out of the hotel to do something together. They needed to stay active. They needed to do something to underscore the fact that they were friends only.

He slipped into jeans and a t-shirt and went into the dining area just in time to hear a knock at the door.

As Gabe opened the door the aroma of cooked eggs and hot coffee greeted him. "Hmm that smells good. We can put it here." Gabe moved the newspapers and his laptop off the table to make room for Maria to set down the trays.

Rory came over to the table picking up lids that covered the plates breathing deeply of the aroma. "Thank you so much Maria."

"Si. You're welcome. Will there be anything else?" Maria looked from Rory to him, her eyes a nervous flutter.

"Just one more thing. Do you know how we could get today's schedule for the boat that takes guests whale watching today?" Gabe looked over at Rory and her bright smile convinced him this would be fun.

"Si. My uncle Jose Moreno runs one of the whale watching boats for tourists." Maria pulled out a piece of paper from her apron pocket. "Here it says today he takes people at ten in the morning and two in the afternoon."

"Hmm... your uncle runs the touring boat. Are your families from the same village then?"

"My village is only an hour away. It's a small seaside village called Pipa. I work here to help out my family." Maria lowered her head.

"That's something to be proud of Maria." Gabe noticed Rory's gentle words took away any sting of awkwardness.

"And we'll be sure to tell your uncle you recommended his whale watching boat." Gabe smiled and nodded.

"Si thank you. Oh and bring warm clothes. It's chilly on the water." Maria nodded and just as quickly backed out of the room closing the door behind her.

"That's great that Maria's uncle runs the tourist boat."

"It is. I'm just wondering why Maria looked a little afraid. Did you notice that?" Rory stood there staring at the closed door for a moment before she turned to look at him.

Gabe thought about it for a minute. "She does seem nervous. I assumed that's because we're new here and she's just getting to know us."

Rory tilted her head to the side her brow puckered in worry. "No, I have a gut feeling it's more than that. Maybe next time I see her I'll have a chance to get to know her better."

"Good idea." Gabe pulled out a chair at the table for Rory just as his stomach rumbled. He chuckled. "For now we'll eat. We have just enough time to eat and get to the whale watching boat this morning."

By the time they finished their breakfast, changed into jeans and walked down to the marina, it was time for the boating to begin.

As they approached the Port there were a few large boats waiting in the harbor. Some had just left the area filled with tourists and only a couple of boats remained waiting for last minute stragglers to show up.

Gabe talked to workers who were wearing the orange vest of the tour guide. Finally he found the man he was looking for.

"Jose Moreno?"

"Si. You want to go see the whales?" He was a short stocky man with a deep olive complexion and a big smile.

"Yes. Your niece Maria recommended you as our tour guide."

At Maria's name the older man chuckled. "Si, Maria is my niece. She's a good girl. Her papa no understand why she hasn't been home in two years. Maria says she's too busy but she will go home yet." His smile wavered a little and then pointed to the boat. "You want to see the whales?"

"Yes, I think we are ready. Rory?" Gabe held out his hand to Rory and they walked toward the dock. After they slipped on their lifejackets they stepped onto the large boat. There were eight other men, women and children who talked excitedly as they waited for the boat to start moving.

Rory sat beside Gabe and squirmed in excitement. Her wide-eyed gaze searched the water and shoreline as the boat moved along the coast. She pointed suddenly to the shore. "Look there's the sea lions."

Gabe saw the light brown animals as they moved slowly along the beach. Not too far away from them were a colony of cormorant birds and a cluster of penguins.

"I love looking at penguins. It looks like they're always wearing tuxedos and ready to go to a party." Rory giggled beside him.

"Yeah, they definitely look cute." Gabe agreed.

Unexpectedly, Jose Moreno stopped the engine. They were far from the coast with the Atlantic ocean all around them. For a moment there was silence only interrupted by the sounds of penguins, seagulls, and cormorants.

Rory grabbed his hand. He looked down to see her violet eyes widen as she pointed to the water other side of the boat. Their whole group was quiet for a moment.

Gabe heard a clicking sound and then a whistling noise as something silvery and white jumped out of the water near the boat. A loud splash startled them all as the whale's body landed with a thud back into the ocean.

"That's just beautiful." Rory whispered beside him. He squeezed her hand loving her excited response to the sight. She held up her smart phone and took several pictures of the whales and a few of them together. "Look there's dolphins jumping and playing beside the whales too."

Two of the children on board with them looked where Rory pointed and got all excited shouting at the whales in the water. Soon everyone was laughing and speaking all at once.

Gabe enjoyed having Rory at his side for the full hour their boat drifted on the water. All too soon their tour guide started the boat's engine and they headed back to shore.

"Thank you for the wonderful tour." Rory spoke to Maria's Uncle.

Gabe shook his hand and asked him about his village. "Do you have people who harvest seaweed and other plants in your village?"

"Si, a few families."

"My wife and I are interested in finding seaweed and other plants that would help my wife make skincare creams. Do you know of some people who would be interested in being our guide to show us the sea plants near your village?" Gabe asked.

"Si. Come tomorrow morning at nine. I will meet you at the red library building on the corner of main-street. You can follow me from there." Jose grinned and shook his hand.

"Thank you. We'll be there." Gabe nodded and grabbed Rory's hand as they drove back to the Resort.

Rory looked at him strangely.

"What? I just wanted to get going on this project. I'm sure Jose knows people who would know where to find the best spots for sea plants and the brown marine algae you need." Gabe squeezed her hand. "It's okay. We'll figure this out together."

Rory sighed. "I know it will be okay. I think I'm just admiring how you simply decide and go after something that you want. That's something I could learn from you. I tend to be shy and slightly timid about asking anyone for help."

He could see the uncertainty in her large eyes. "Maybe it would help if you talked to Jose and the others tomorrow. That might really help you to feel more courageous and help you get the answers you need for this project."

"Maybe." She hesitated and he quirked an eyebrow at her. "Okay you're right. I will do the talking tomorrow."

Gabe was learning new things about Rory. He made a mental note to continue to help his wife and encourage her to do things beyond what she believed she was capable of doing.

Soon after they arrived back at the Resort they went to their suite and showered and changed into clean clothes.

Since the weather had turned unusually hot for this time of year he changed into shorts and a t-shirt ready to enjoy some sun.

Rory stood waiting for him by the door. She wore a dark purple t-shirt and white shorts. The combination made her violet eyes stand out and emphasized her slim, tanned legs.

His wife was beautifully formed.

Gabe quickly returned his gaze to her face and reminded himself that no matter how big the temptation he should not be gawking at Rory.

"Should we try out one of those restaurants in the main area of the resort?"

"Sounds good." Gabe followed her downstairs to the large main area and they were soon seated at a nice Italian restaurant.

As they waited for their food they sipped water for a moment before Rory spoke. "When you talked to Maria's uncle today he said her papa was sad that she hadn't been home in two years because she'd been too busy with work. What do you make of that?"

Gabe chuckled a little at his wife. "Rory you sure are

concerned about Maria. Maybe there's nothing to make of it at all. Maybe she really is too busy to go home."

Rory scowled a little at him. "I don't know about that. And yes I am concerned about Maria. Call it a gut feeling but I believe not everything is as it should be in her life."

"Okay fine. I adore the fact that you are very compassionate toward others Rory." Gabe smiled at the waiter who brought their plates of food.

"Thank you." Rory replied with a warmth in her tone that was lacking before.

"Maybe you could ask her mother or one of her brothers or sisters tomorrow. I think Jose plans to take us to Maria's family home in Pipa."

"I guess I could." Rory conceded.

After a refreshing meal they both agreed that some time sitting in the sun would be ideal. They went to their suite to grab their swimsuits and towels and soon found a lovely quiet spot poolside.

Gabe saw Rory reach into her beach bag pulling out a book. He grabbed a book too. "What are you reading?"

"I love reading romances so I brought along a new novel by one of my favorite authors." Rory peered over at the book in his hands and her eyes widened. "Are you reading one of the books I wrote?"

Gabe chuckled at her surprised look. "I thought I should. Maybe I'll get to know some of your secrets that way."

He could see a stain of red starting on her neck that quickly rose to her cheeks. "This is the first book in your Island romance series and I thought since you spent most of your childhood on Walker's Island this story would be a great starting place."

Gabe leafed through the front pages of the book. "Besides, the dedication of the book really piques my interest: *To the one man who started my love of romance in the first place.* I'd love to know who you dedicated this book to."

Gabe glanced up from the book hoping his wife would answer him only to be surprised when she stood to her feet beside her lounge chair. Hurrying she put her t-shirt on over her bathing suit. "I'm sorry. I forgot something from our room. I have to go. Be back soon."

Puzzled Gabe watched his wife as she hurried across the poolside deck and disappeared through the doors that led to the elevators.

What was so important that she had to dash off so quickly? Was it something he said?

One thing he knew for sure, he still had a lot to learn about his fake wife.

RORY'S LEGS and arms shook in the elevator all the way up to the top floor to their suite of rooms.

She was so shook up that Gabe — her best friend since she was six years old — was reading one of her romances.

Opening the door to their room she closed it quickly and leaned her head against the door.

Did Gabe have to choose that series to read? That was the series where she had poured so much of her romantic imaginings of how it could be if Gabe would fall in love with her. It was her love for Gabe that had got her started writing romance in the first place. That's what had inspired the dedication to that book, but she wasn't about to tell him that.

She walked across the room and poured herself a glass of water. Her hands were still shaking from his almost discovery of one of her biggest secrets.

And she did need to keep her love for Gabe Stevenson a secret. They might be married but it was a fake marriage. If he found out she loved him most likely he would believe she was manipulating him. That was the last thing she wanted him to think of her.

No, her love for her husband would have to remain a secret. Though how she would do that she had no clue. Each day he was so nice to her. He had thoughtfully figured out a way that she could get more of those sea plants that she so desperately needed to make the formula for her organic skin creams.

All these thoughtful and generous acts that Gabe did also made her realize more and more that he wasn't the selfish man she'd believed he'd become over the years.

She had thought that the money and fame would have changed him into someone who could no longer appreciate the little things or the little people. But that didn't appear to be what happened to Gabe.

He had changed but he had done his best to become a better man.

Rory took another long drink of water and walked toward the window that looked down to the pools. For a moment she watched her husband as he relaxed on with his nose in a book.

She would need to keep her guard up or Gabe would find out her horrible secret.

She was in love with him.

Her husband only wanted to be married for one year. She wanted to be married for a lifetime. He held himself back from falling in love. She longed to fall in love.

It was an impossible situation.

She didn't know how long she stood there thinking until she finally remembered Gabe waited for her.

She needed to get back downstairs. Belatedly she remembered telling Gabe she needed to grab something. Spying the sunscreen on the corner of the counter she quickly grabbed it and opened the door.

Stepping into the hallway she overheard a heated conversation. She stopped in her tracks and backed up into the room leaving the door open slightly.

A man's angry voice spoke loudly with a mixture of English and Spanish. Then a familiar woman's voice spoke a rapid volley of words in reply.

Rory caught a little of what they were saying.

She peeked her head out the door and looked down the hallway. Near the end of the hallway she could see a large dark haired man holding Maria's arms in a tight grip.

His face was a mask of anger and his words dripped with contempt. "You... don't have a choice." Maria winced as his fingers seemed to grip her arms harder. "...was our deal... get a job here. Now I want you to do more... no choice."

Rory put her hand to her mouth and she sucked in a breath. Was the man forcing Maria to do something she didn't want to do? Did he have some kind of control over her?

"No... not agree." Maria tried to pull away from the man but he held tightly to her arm. Rory could hear the desperation and panic in Maria's voice.

"You will do this... or big trouble." The man jerked her arms one more time then suddenly let go. He hurried away from Maria and Rory could hear her hushed sobs. When the man disappeared down the elevator Rory stepped out into the hallway and hurried over to Maria.

Maria saw her coming and hurried to dry her tears. "Mrs. Stevenson sorry. You need me for something?"

"No I don't need anything. Are you are okay?" Rory hoped Maria would tell her something.

"Si. I'm good. I should get back to work."

Rory spoke quickly as the maid started to move away. "Wait please." She pressed needing to know what was going on. "I overheard some of what that man said to you. He was forcing you to do something you didn't want to do. Is he your boss? What's his name?"

Maria glanced away for a moment. Looking down she spoke. "Si, he's my boss. His name is Carlos Santos. But I can't tell you what he's doing. He would hurt my family." She started picking up supplies from the cart she pushed. "I'm late. I have to go."

"Maria we will help you. We can help you get away from this man and stop him from hurting your family." Rory whispered passionately hoping that her new friend would listen.

"No one can help me now. It's too late. I must go." Maria hurriedly pushed her cart down the hallway.

Rory stared at the retreating maid. Sadness hovered over her and she wished there was something she could do. Just then the elevator doors opened and Gabe stepped out.

"There you are. I thought you were coming back." Gabe walked toward her the corners of his mouth turned up with mischief until he looked at her closely. He put one finger under her chin and looked into her eyes that shimmered with unshed tears. "Rory, what's wrong?"

Rory quickly wiped away the tears that had formed as she continued to think of Maria's situation.

"Oh Gabe I'm so sad about Maria." Rory continued and explained to him about what she'd overheard. "It's like he's threatening her. And Maria told me that if she tells me what's going on that man will hurt her family. I'm really worried about her. Is there anything we can do to help?"

Gabe caught a stray tear with his thumb. It had slipped out of the corner of one eye unnoticed. His eyes crinkled as his blue gaze focused on hers. "Ah Rory you really do have a soft heart. It's one of the things I adore about you."

Warmth stirred in her belly at his words and she averted her gaze for a moment. Forcing a relaxed smile Rory spoke. "Thank you, but I'm really worried about our maid. Is there something we can do to help Maria?"

"Yes. I'll call a friend who'll be able to look into it." Gabe reassured her and Rory blew out a small breath of relief.

"Okay. Good." She nodded feeling better.

"Why don't you head down to the swimming pool area and I'll make that call. I'll join you soon." Gabe walked with her to the elevator and she waved at him as the doors closed.

Walking toward the poolside lounge area her thoughts turned to Gabe. The very fact that he was willing to take his time and money to help someone he barely knew who was in need spoke well of him.

Her husband was fast becoming a hero in her eyes.

Rory was growing attached and more in love with her fake husband. She didn't know how to stop these feelings that were blossoming more and more with each day she spent with him.

Did she even want to?

৯

"Hey Max? Gabe Stevenson here."

"What's up?"

"I have a name I'd like you to investigate. His name is Carlos Santos. He's been threatening one of the workers here and I'm wondering what we can do to stop him." Gabe explained more details about the situation.

"I'd like to fly you and some key people on your team to investigate more about what's going on with this guy. Would that work for you?"

"Yes. I'll first do a little background check on this guy. I'll be there tomorrow morning with two guys from my team." Max's crisp business-like tone set Gabe's mind at ease.

"Great. Thanks Max." Gabe turned his phone off and set it in his case beside his bed.

As he headed out the door and down the elevator he

thought of Rory. His childhood friend had become someone whom he realized was not like other women he knew.

Rory had a compassion for others who were in pain unlike anyone he knew except maybe his own Mom. His new wife was fast becoming one of the most important people in his life.

He was beginning to like her far more than he thought possible. He was beginning to like her far more than he should.

It was confusing.

How could he stop these growing feelings for his fake wife?

CHAPTER NINE

ory

JOSE MORENO WAVED at them as Gabe parked the vehicle by the red building on the corner of main street.

Rory stepped out and looked around the small seaside village.

Buildings of all different colors and sizes were all around her. There were signs in Spanish as well as a teashop and a church with a Welsh name. It was great to see people from so many different backgrounds living in harmony together in one village.

Gabe placed a gentle hand on the small of her back as she walked beside him.

"Good you're here." Jose shook their hands and waved for them to follow. "Come I take you to Maria's family's place. You will see a lot of sea plants."

"Sounds great. Thank you Jose." Rory remembered what Gabe had said about her learning how to be more courageous when she spoke to others. At least she was trying.

It was a short walk between trees and small houses until they stopped at a small yellow house. It was a simple flat board home square in shape with only a few windows.

As they arrived Jose called out, "Pedro you home?"

A man very similar in height and build to Jose stepped out the door followed by a woman with greying hair who stood by his side.

Five children quickly scampered out the door behind their parents. The oldest three boys seemed like they were between the ages of twelve to sixteen and the two youngest girls seemed like they were much younger. They ran to hug their mother.

"These two guests come from resort where Maria is. They are interested in sea plants." Jose explained.

Rory stepped forward to shake their hands and Gabe did the same.

"You see my Maria?" The mother asked Rory.

"Yes she has been a great help to us." Rory didn't explain all that was going on because she didn't want to worry Maria's mother.

Gabe's private investigator had arrived just before they left the resort this morning. Max Harrington was going to talk to the police. Hopefully Carlos, the man who had been threatening Maria, would soon be behind bars.

"You have a wonderful daughter Mrs. Moreno."

"*Gracias.* Call me Lucia." She waved Rory to follow her. They walked past the hill and down toward the rocky beach and the ocean's edge. "If you want sea plants you have come to the right place."

Lucia took her to a large inlet where there was a vast amount of seaweed, marine algae and other sea plants. Maria's mother pulled seaweed and brown marine algae from along the waters edge.

Rory held it in her hands and a wide grin stretched the corners of her mouth.

"It's perfect and so pure. There is so much here." Rory could hardly believe her eyes as she looked around her. It was just what she needed.

"You want?"

"Yes, very much." Rory realized this was her chance to ask for the help she needed. With a quick look at Gabe who nodded at her, she looked back at Lucia.

The children crowded close as she asked, "Could I hire you and your family to hand-harvest these sea plants? I'm looking for a group of people or a family who would be willing to do this every month. I would pay you well. Maybe you could talk to your husband and see if that's something your family would like to do."

Lucia glanced at her husband and Spanish words flew back and forth between them. Her husband shrugged as if to say it was up to his wife. "Si. We will do this."

"Oh thank you. My husband Gabe and I will get the contract written and then we will set things up properly." Rory spoke to Lucia who nodded. They started walking back to the house.

They were just about to leave when Lucia's troubled brown eyes stared into hers. "Please tell Maria her mama longs for her to come home."

MELODY ARCHER

Rory could feel the heavy burden Maria's mother carried for her children. "I promise to talk to her and ask her to come see you."

Lucia squeezed her hand tightly once more and put her hand to her heart. Her brown eyes were filled with tears and Rory squeezed her hand. It was an unspoken heartfelt gesture that each of them understood.

They waved goodbye and hurried back to the waiting jeep.

It was only after they had driven for a few minutes in silence that Gabe spoke. "Rory you amaze me. Not only were you able to negotiate a contract for the supplies you need for your skin care products, but from those tears in Lucia's eyes, it was like she trusted and connected with you quickly."

Rory shrugged. "Maybe it's a woman to woman thing. I can't imagine how difficult it must be for her as a mom not to see her child for years. As I talked with Maria's mom my own memories of the pain and heartache of growing up without my parents hit me hard again. In that moment I realized I would do whatever I could to help Lucia and Maria to be reunited again."

Gabe nodded slightly. "Like I said you're amazing."

"Thanks Gabe." Rory warmed at his words. She could admit that having her husband compliment her felt wonderful. If he appreciated her did that mean love was possible?

She didn't know but a small flare of hope was kindled which she kept hidden in her heart of hearts.

Rory and Gabe drove onto the parking lot only to see

two police cruisers parked at odd angles in front of the main building of the Resort.

They had just stepped out of the jeep when the doors opened and two policemen walked out of the building each holding onto Carlos Santos arms.

Carlos was handcuffed and spewed angry words as they led him down the stairs into the waiting police cruiser.

Max Harrison followed close behind standing on the steps as the police drove away with Carlos Santos.

"Come let's see what Max has to say." Gabe reached for her hand as they walked toward the front entrance.

As soon as Max spotted them he hurried over. "As you probably saw we managed to find enough dirt on Carlos for him to spend time behind bars for years. We discovered multiple incidents of human trafficking. That was what he was forcing Maria and a few other girls at the Resort to be involved in. Not only did he force them to give him half of their wages but he also threatened to harm their families if they said anything."

"That's terrible." Rory sucked in air horrified that something like that had happened to Maria.

"Turns out that's not the only thing we found. Carlos was also involved in trafficking illegal drugs as well as humans. Needless to say the police will have enough to hold him in jail for a very long time." Max grinned.

Gabe nodded. "Good." He looked over at Rory. "Maria and the other girls will be safe now that Carlos has been caught."

Rory nodded and her body shivered at what they'd

discovered about Carlos. She was just grateful Maria was safe. "I need to find her and ask if she's okay."

She started to walk forward but Max spoke suddenly. "Before you go, I wanted to let you both know that my team found some fingerprints at the site of the fire on Walker's Island. We're in the process of checking out what've found and we should have some answers in the next day or two."

Rory looked from Max to Gabe swallowing back fear that coiled in her belly. She nodded and her hand shook as she toyed with a long strand of hair. "Good. Thanks." Why was her voice suddenly so strained?

Max's phone rang loudly startling her. Max looked at the caller ID and spoke to Gabe. "I need to take this. Talk to you soon."

"Of course. Thanks Max. We look forward to hearing what you've found." Gabe stepped beside her and slipped his arm around her waist. "Come, we'll go up to our suite. You're looking slightly wobbly on feet."

Gabe walked close by her side into the Resort.

As the elevator doors opened to their floor, Rory saw Maria pushing her cart down the hallway.

"I need to talk to her. I'll be back soon." Rory hurried down the hallway.

"Maria." Rory called out to the maid who stopped and turned. "Thank you for stopping to talk. I just wanted to ask if you heard the news that Carlos was arrested?"

"Si, I did. I'm very happy." It was the first time since she'd met Maria that Rory saw a bright smile free of worry and fear.

"I'm glad. You deserve to be happy Maria." Rory

noticed the maid's smile was hesitant as if unsure. "And I wanted to tell you that I went to visit your parents to ask if your family would consider harvesting sea plants for my skin care products and they said yes."

"That's real good." Maria nodded her eyes pensive as if pondering what that would all mean for her family.

"But the best part is your mama asked you to come home. She misses you as does your whole family." Rory looked at her, hoping she wasn't overstepping her boundaries by acting as the middle person.

"Si. Now I am free to go home. Carlos no more can hurt me or my family." Her brown eyes brimmed with tears and she quickly wiped them away.

"I'm so happy for you Maria." Impulsively Rory gave the maid a big hug. "My husband and I will be leaving tomorrow but we'll be back soon. I look forward to seeing you again. You are free now. Go and be happy Maria."

Maria nodded a big smile on her lovely face. Rory turned and went back to their hotel room, feeling so happy that things had turned out well for Maria.

Entering their room Rory collapsed onto the sofa. Her mind was still spinning with both Maria and Max's news.

However, it was Max's news that they were close to finding out the identity of the person that started the fire on the Island that disturbed her most.

Wrapping her arms around herself she tried to calm her queasy stomach.

"Talk to me Rory." Gabe sat down beside her and slipped his strong arms around her pulling her close. His warm breath whispered softly into her ear. "You're worried about who Max and his team will identify as the person who started that fire aren't you?"

She looked up at him her eyes wide wondering how he could've read her mind. "How did you know that?"

"Because I know you my beautiful water sprite."

Rory offered him a small smile. "You haven't called me that in years."

"I know. You don't mind?" Gabe's blue eyes sparkled with a little bit of mischief.

"No I don't mind. I have fond memories of those summers we spent together." She smiled trying to lighten the mood but her thoughts kept returning to the trouble they had on the Island.

He chuckled beside her the rumbling in his chest a comforting sound to Rory. He sat silent for a moment and then put a finger under her chin tipping it up so he could look deeply into her eyes. "But on a more serious note I think I've learned a little something about you. Want to know what I think?"

"I'm all ears."

"I think you believe that the person they will discover started the fire at your aunts' cottage is someone that you knew and loved when you were a child. And that terrifies you." Gabe lifted her blond hair away from her eyes searching for the truth.

Tears formed in her eyes and spilled down her cheeks. "It's true. I'm very afraid that I won't recover from what I find when the truth comes out. What can I do Gabe? How do I get through this?"

"We'll do this together. When they uncover the truth

I'll be right there beside you." There was a tender warmth in her husband's eyes.

"Promise?" A few more stray tears edged out of the corners of her eyes as she looked up at him.

Just for that moment she was six years old again filled with fear asking him if he would keep his promise to marry her if she was still afraid when she grew up.

She'd been so scared when she'd first moved the Island. The horror of the loss of her parents and the only home she'd ever known had made her fear almost everything and everyone around her.

Except Gabe.

He'd been so gentle and kind to her that she had attached herself to him and followed him around from the first day she saw him.

Gabe been the brother she never had. At least until she grew to be a teenager when her feelings had blossomed into more.

But now her husband only wanted a fake relationship — he only wanted to be friends — and it confused her when he was so gentle and lover-like. Similar to how he was acting now.

She blinked and her eyes widened as he leaned his head close to hers.

"I promise." Gabe's gentle fingers wiped tears that had fallen down her cheeks. His eyes darkened to a deep blue and he stared at her for a moment before he lowered his head and touched gentle lips to hers.

The caress of his lips on hers ignited an explosion of butterflies in her belly. Tingles of awareness surged up her arms and she placed her hands around her husband's neck. For Rory suddenly her world had gone from many shades of grey to being lit up with all the colors of the rainbow.

She leaned closer to her husband, each touch of their lips kindling a growing passion.

Without warning Gabe's phone started ringing startling them both.

Gabe reluctantly pulled his lips from hers, his blue eyes darkened like a stormy sea. He looked at the caller ID. "I'm sorry but I've got to take this call. It might be important."

Dazed she nodded. Gabe's voice trailed off as he disappeared with his phone into his room.

Already she missed his closeness.

Her husband was fast becoming the one person she longed to be with all the time.

She hoped they would only grow closer when they returned back home to the Island. Was that possible?

CHAPTER TEN

abe

As HIS PRIVATE jet circled over Walker's Island Gabe looked down to the surface below pleased that his great-grandfather's Island was now his own.

He had his new wife-in-name-only to thank for this huge blessing in his life.

Turning, he peered over at Rory who sat reading a book on her seat across the table. She was so beautiful and — he was beginning to realize — a real temptation for him.

Yesterday when they got back to the hotel he would have gladly continued kissing her sweet lips if not for that phone call. However it wasn't only her outward beauty that drew her to him it was her inward beauty and compassion.

The way she had helped Maria and how she had bravely talked to Maria's family about partnering with her in the skincare business was admirable.

He discovered a new side to his childhood friend that was incredible. He admired her for not avoiding what was happening with Maria but for trying to figure out a solution.

None of the other women he dated would have cared enough to try to help someone else like that. From his experience they would've thought that someone who served them wasn't worth their attention.

Clearly he'd been wrong about a few assumptions he'd made about Rory. He could admit that.

Yet, he couldn't forget that she was only his fake wife.

He needed to try to refocus and get back to the deal they agreed on.

The harder he tried the more difficult it became to hold himself back from kissing her senseless. His wife was becoming more and more irresistible to him.

How was he supposed to keep treating her like a sister when he definitely didn't have brotherly feelings towards her?

He needed a way to show Rory his good intentions.

"Rory do you want a bird's eye view of Walker's Island? Take a look out the window." Gabe pointed below to the view they could see from their shared window. "Can you see to the South of Grand's Hunting Lodge?"

"Yes. I see it."

"That building they are constructing is going to be a

small hotel for workers who work at the Hotel and Resort." Gabe then pointed farther south. "See those red flags in the ground that span a large U shaped area?"

"Yes."

"The general contractor for this project staked out the land area needed to build a very large resort. And in that middle piece of land we'll build a few varied sized swimming pools for adults and kids. Oh and we'll add a health spa in there somewhere." Gabe looked over at Rory whose eyes were glued below. "So what do you think?"

She turned to him her eyes beaming and a smile hovering on her lips. "I think it's really great. Gabe you've put in a lot of work planning all this. I'm glad you showed me from way up here. Now I feel like I have a better perspective. "

"Yeah it'll be good. The hardest part is getting the workers to stay and work on a quiet Island that has no shops and very few people." Gabe rubbed the back of his neck. "Not exactly sure how to deal with that problem but we're working on it."

Rory put a finger on her chin a sure sign she was thinking. "You could appeal to people's adventurous side. Promote it as a once in a lifetime adventure. That would inspire more workers to come to the Island."

"You might be on to something. I'll have Darby my Human Resources manager look into that idea." Gabe grinned.

The plane descended onto the landing strip and before long they were walking the trail toward Grand's Hunting Lodge.

The loud blast of his private jet taking off surrounded

them. Gabe had told his pilot and co-pilot to go ahead and fly to Seattle's airport to spend time with their families.

He wouldn't need to fly again for a little while. His jet needed its routine mechanical inspection anyway so leaving the airplane in the Stevenson private hangar would be ideal.

Gabe's gaze rested on Rory as they approached Grand's Lodge. He still thought of this large home as Grand's special place even though the Island and the home belonged to him now.

This would be the first time he was bringing Rory home as Mrs. Stevenson. The thought made him happy. He would hire a housekeeper and cook soon, preferably someone who wouldn't mind living in the small guest-house behind the Hunting Lodge.

He liked that idea. That way they would have someone to cook and clean and Rory would have more time to write and formulate her skin care products and he'd have more time too. It was ideal.

She was always helping others maybe it was time his wife had someone to help her.

As he walked up to the door he remembered how his great-grandfather said when you marry, treat your wife like a princess and always have nice surprises up your sleeve.

As they approached the front door Gabe thought now was as good a time as any to listen to Grand.

Stopping suddenly, he let go of the two suitcases he pulled alongside. Placing one hand around Rory's waist and one under her legs he lifted her up in his arms.

"Gabe what are you doing?" Rory gasped and her jaw dropped open in surprise.

He chuckled as he opened the large wood door. "Grand always told me when I married to treat my bride like a princess. So I thought carrying you across the threshold would be a step in the right direction."

Rory giggled as he carried her through the open door and into the wide entryway of the Hunting Lodge. Gabe's smile grew bigger.

He loved Rory's contagious laugh. He could listen to it all day.

Slowly he slid his wife down against his body. Her pink mouth turned up at the corners into an enchanting smile. Those lips held such fond memories. Rory made him come alive in ways he never thought possible.

For a moment he didn't even think but just pulled her close leaning down to press his lips against hers. An explosion of moist warmth — the kind with a strong strawberry flavor like his Grandmom's strawberry short-cake — met his lips and in that moment he had the strongest sense that he'd come home.

His thoughts spiraled.

This couldn't be happening with Rory his childhood friend. She was like a friend and sister all rolled into one.

Just as suddenly as he kissed her, he took a step back. His hands shook a little as nervous jitters hit him.

Somewhere along the way the importance of his wife in his life had shifted. She now meant more to him than he ever thought possible.

He didn't know how to deal with that. Running his

fingers through his hair he changed the subject. "Ah, I'm going to bring in our suitcases."

Rory nodded quickly, her violet eyes wide and uncertain.

With hurried steps he walked out the door to get the suitcases feeling like the worst kind of husband.

Confusion gnawed at him and he wondered if he would ever be able to figure out himself or exactly what was happening between him and his fake wife?

§♠

SHE STOOD THERE MOTIONLESS, touching gentle fingers to her lips.

Gabe had surprised her again with his passionate kisses.

Kisses that had made her go weak in the knees. Just when she had wanted her husband's embrace to go on forever he'd suddenly pulled away.

He confused and frustrated her all at the same time. Yet her heart still longed to be close him. She wanted to experience more of her husband's kisses and to know and understand his heart.

Rory expelled a long breath.

She didn't know if what she longed for would ever happen. But she knew she would remain hopeful. Maybe he just needed a little more time to trust her fully. Rory reassured herself that if it took more time that was okay.

They had a year together.

Maybe by the time the year was over their fake marriage would turn into something real.

Meanwhile Rory would do her best to make this house a home.

Turning she started down the hallway toward the large open kitchen. To her surprise she saw a massive card planted on the rustic wood table.

Gabe's footsteps echoed on the wood floor behind her. "It looks like it's from my family."

Rory read the card out loud. *Congratulations to the happy couple. A little birdie told us that you would be coming to Cyrus and Anna Noble's Benefit Gala on Friday next week. We would like to ask Rory if she'd like to spend time with us girls at the spa and shopping for the day? Please let us know. Love Mom, Elle and Bella and your Grandmom.*

"That's very thoughtful of them to include me." Rory looked at Gabe.

"Yes it was." Gabe set down the card. "Sorry I forgot to mention the Benefit Gala next Friday evening. Cyrus asked me to speak. Will you come with me to the benefit?"

Rory eyed Gabe feeling a little uncomfortable with the thought of being in a room full of people who were so cultured and wealthy. She was just the barefoot Island girl.

How would she ever fit in?

She tucked a stray hair behind her ear and licked her lips nervously. "Yes if you want me there of course I'll join you."

"Of course I want you there with me. You'll shine like a rare jewel in a vast sea of plastic cut-outs." His rogue smile was back. While she appreciated his compliment she didn't share his confidence.

"But I don't have any kind of formal evening dress to wear." Rory hugged her arms around herself. If Gabe knew what her wardrobe looked like she was convinced he'd want to hide from embarrassment.

"From the invitation on this card it looks like my family has decided to take care of that with an afternoon of shopping. Would you like to join them?" Gabe asked like it was the most normal thing in the world.

Despite being scared to enter a world that she knew nothing of, the need to please her husband and new family was greater. "Yes, I think I would."

"Good. I think you'll have fun Rory. And make sure you buy not only an evening dress but any other clothes or accessories that you need without looking at the price. I have credit cards and a bankcard set up in your name so no excuses. Promise me you'll do this?" Gabe stood there with his arms crossed in front of him, his blue eyes focused on hers like a laser beam. He knew her well.

"I promise." Rory realized had entered a new world. A world where she didn't need to focus on how much things cost.

For the first time she would be able to shop for clothes and get what she liked. "I will ask your Mom, Grandmom and Elle and Bella for advice on what to buy so you can be proud to have me at your side."

Gabe shook his head. "I'm always proud to have you on my arm Rory." He looked like he was about to say something else but stopped.

"Thanks Gabe." She turned to look around the room. "Well if you could show me to my room I'll unpack my clothes."

Her husband grabbed their suitcases and headed down the long wide hallway. The rustic feel of the timber frame

Lodge with its overhead beam made her feel tiny and humble in the midst of all this vastness.

She had a feeling this was only the beginning.

"Here's your bedroom. Mine is right across the hall." He opened the large wood door and waited for her to enter. Rory walked inside loving the light colors on the walls. "This used to be my great-grandmother's room. Grand wanted to make sure my great-grandmother had all the space she needed when he built the house."

"It's beautiful and about three times the size of my room at the cottage." She looked up at him pleased that he'd given her this room. "I'll unpack and than make us a meal."

"About that." Gabe put a finger on his chin. "I was thinking we could go to the cottage and visit your aunts. They would be pleased to see you."

Rory grinned excited at that idea. "Okay. Let me just get this organized and then we can go."

Gabe chuckled and left her to her task.

It wasn't too long before she had changed into her comfy jeans and sweatshirt and went to meet Gabe. Rory carried a small bag of gifts she'd bought for her aunts from their trip.

"It wouldn't surprise me if Aunt Florrie has food already waiting. She's always cooking something." Soon they were on Gabe's ATV and driving down the trail toward the cottage.

Aunt Merrie ran out to meet them. "Welcome you two lovebirds. You came just in time. Aunt Florrie has just finished making the soup. Come in and sit by the table."

Rory quirked an eyebrow at Gabe as if to say I told you so.

As they sat around the kitchen table they said grace and started eating. Rory told them about their adventures from their trip to Argentina. "Oh my I'm glad the man was caught and sent to jail and that those girls and you both were safe." Aunt Fawn said softly shaking her head.

"We were all fine Auntie. And it turns out Maria's family was willing to work with me to help hand harvest sea plants so that I can formulate larger quantities of the skin creams." At their curious looks Rory explained. "It was Gabe's idea and he encouraged me to get the help I need."

"Good Gabe. And Rory we're excited for you. I know so many of our friends and other people from Paradise Lake's weekly craft fairs have been asking when you would have more jars available. This is perfect." Aunt Merrie said.

"It was all Rory's doing. She's a force to be reckoned with." Gabe winked a Rory and she could feel warmth hitting her cheeks from his attention.

Ever the practical one, Aunt Florrie shook her head as she pointed out the big obstacle in this new plan. "How is Rory going to have the time to write, mix the formula for her skin care and cook and clean that large house? It's too much."

"I'm glad you brought that up Aunt Florrie. I've wanted to ask you if there is anyone you trust that you would recommend as a housekeeper and cook for us? She could live in the three bedroom guest house for free and we'd pay her well."

Rory looked over at her husband surprised. It seemed that as usual Gabe was a step ahead.

"I know of someone. She and I go way back and I would trust her with my life." Aunt Merrie grinned and clapped her hands together. "Her name is Betty O'Toole. She's my age, widowed with three married children who live across the country. She's lonely and this would be perfect for her. Plus she'd be close by and could come to tea ever so often."

Her three aunts nodded and looked at Gabe.

"Rory what do you say? Is that a good idea?" Rory smiled happy that he'd thought to ask her. "Yes I've meet Mrs. O'Toole and she's a kind warm-hearted person. I think she would be a great cook."

"Good. I can call and see if we can get that settled this week then."

Aunt Merrie spoke up. "I can call Betty if you'd like? I can explain what you're offering and then if she has questions Betty can talk to Rory."

Finishing their meal, Aunt Florrie boiled water to make tea.

"That sounds good." Gabe toyed with his cup.

"I'm glad you're boiling the water for tea Aunt Florrie. It reminds me of the present we brought back for you three. Some traditional Argentina Mate herb tea along with a gourd to use to pour the tea into." Rory pulled out the yellow gourd she had in her backpack and the numerous bags of tealeaves she had brought home with her.

"Rory this is wonderful. Let's try it." Aunt Merrie was always in the mood to try something new. Soon Aunt

Florrie was pouring the boiling water into the yellow gourd and the Mate herb tea lingered at the top.

"Tradition says you're supposed to pass the tea around to each person. It's supposed to be a way of welcoming people to your home." Rory could see the doubtful expressions on her aunts' faces but they were willing to give it a try.

"It's a little bitter." Aunt Merrie added honey and they all agreed it was a little easier to swallow.

"Speaking of presents we have something for you Rory. We wanted to give you a birthday gift a little early." Aunt Fawn nodded to Aunt Merrie who hurried up the stairs and returned carrying a bunch of tattered notebooks.

She handed them to Rory and said, "These are your Mother's journals. She started writing them when she was a teenager. The last entry was dated the day before your sixth birthday party."

Rory eyes moistened. A few tears slipped down her cheeks as she stared at the torn edges of the multi-colored notebooks. "These are my Mom's words." She breathed out. So many questions filled her that she wasn't even sure where to start.

"We didn't feel like you were ready to read them until you were an adult Rory. That's why we waited so long. We didn't mean to hurt you by holding them back. Once you read the diaries you might agree that many of the personal things that your Mom wrote in her diary were better left for adult ears only." Aunt Merrie spoke softly. "We hope you're not too upset at us."

Rory reached a hand over to her aunt and squeezed it.

"No I'm not upset. You were protecting me." Rory held the journals close to her heart. "Thank you for this. Maybe some of the questions I have will be answered as I read her words."

"I hope so my dear." Aunt Fawn patted her hand.

Aunt Florrie spoke quickly. "And one more thing."

"Another gift?" Rory asked.

"Well they are yours anyway but we wondered if you'd like to take Mocha and Latte with you? They're your dogs more than ours. We thought we might get a small dog." Aunt Florrie smiled.

"What do you think Gabe?" Rory wanted to respect that it was Gabe's great-grandfather's place and that he was okay with it.

"Sure whatever you want." Gabe chuckled. "I remember Grand had his dogs that he brought to the Island in the summer. I sure had fun with them. It might make the place feel more like home to have your furry friends around." Gabe chuckled.

"Then I'd love that."

A sense of happiness surrounded Rory. She was with Gabe and her aunts and everything felt right in her world. At least for the moment.

The sun started to go down and Rory stood to her feet. "I think we should probably get back. I want to grab my computer and a few things from my bedroom before we go."

Rory hurried upstairs to her room and placed her computer and a few clothes inside her backpack. She looked around her room and realized that it would be a long time before she'd be back.

Now she would live at her husband's home at least for the next year. She felt nervous and excited all at the same time.

Hurrying back downstairs she saw Gabe by the back door talking with Aunt Merrie.

"Latte and Mocha, here boys." Her dogs came quickly and sat on their haunches waiting patiently as she slipped on her shoes. She patted their heads. "They think they're going on a walk to the beach which they love. This will be a new adventure for them."

She was just about to slip on her backpack when Aunt Merrie stopped her. "Here are your mother's journals. There are about twelve of them."

With shaky hands she slipped the journals inside her backpack blinking back tears.

"Thank you Aunt Merrie." Rory kissed her cheek and looked up to see her aunts close by. "Come here you three. Thank you. I'm so grateful for all you've done for me. The good new is we're nearby so this isn't goodbye but simply I'll see you a little later. I will be back regularly to check on you all."

After Rory had hugged and kissed all three of them, she followed Gabe out the door. Her aunts wiped the corners of their eyes and she blew them a kiss. She settled behind Gabe on the ATV.

"Ready to go?" Gabe turned to ask above the noise of the engine. His eyes held a warm compassion that melted her heart, causing a few more tears to slip down her cheeks.

It would be so strange to live with Gabe at the Hunting Lodge now. The location wasn't very far from where she'd grown up at the cottage but it was the fact that she was living in this house as Gabe's wife. Well his fake wife. It was all so new and a far grander lifestyle than she was used to. It made her a little afraid she wouldn't measure up.

But she didn't want to weigh Gabe down with all her worries. So she simply said, "Yes, I'm ready to go."

Rory waved once more to her aunts and they hurried along the trail back to their home. Mocha and Latte followed behind.

With her arms around Gabe some of the worry melted away and she felt comforted. She could trust Gabe — her childhood friend — to help her through this.

As they drove up to the Hunting Lodge Rory spotted a man sitting on the front steps.

Gabe stopped the ATV and turned off the engine.

"Max you're back." Gabe walked forward and shook his hand. Rory did the same. "What brings you by?"

Her body tensed. She was sure Max had learned the identity of the person who started the fire. She braced herself for the worst.

"I wanted to stop by to give you the results of the investigation. We had lab work done for the fingerprints we found on the jars from the fire." Max pulled out his smartphone and searched for his documents.

"Yes. That's good." Gabe turned to her, his blue eyes filled with warmth. He grabbed her hand and squeezed in a comforting grip. Rory gave him a hesitant half smile in return. "What did you find?"

How could her husband sound so calm? She grew anxious and keyed up as she waited for Max's reply.

"The person identified is a man who goes by the name Ned Baxter. He lives in Oregon." Max looked at Rory and then at Gabe. "Does that name ring any bells?"

Rory sighed in relief. "That name is not familiar to me nor have I heard my aunts mention anyone by that name."

"I don't recognize the name at all." Gabe responded. He put a finger on his chin thinking. "That's strange. Here I thought we would uncover a bit of a clue. Do you know anything about this Ned fellow?"

"Yes. It looks like he's a twenty-two year old male who still lives with his Mom. Her name is Nadine Baxter. That's all we have to go on for the moment." Max slipped his smartphone back in his pocket and stood there in silence for a moment.

"Sorry we didn't find anything really useful. My team and I will dig deeper into the background of this Ned fellow as well as his mother. I'll keep you informed of any new developments." Max looked beyond them toward the waterway behind. "We'll keep digging down to the truth that's all I can tell you."

"Appreciate that Max. We just want to put a stop to the senseless attacks against my wife. We have complete faith that you'll find something soon." Gabe shook Max's hand as did Rory and he waved as he walked away.

Rory slid the backpack off her shoulders as they walked toward the house. "I wish we knew more information. Who is Ned Baxter anyway? Never heard of him."

Gabe placed a gentle hand on her back as he opened the door. "I don't know. But Max and his team will find more information soon I'm confident of that." He grabbed her heavy backpack filled with journals and released a small chuckle. "And who knows maybe your Mom left a clue in one of her journals."

"Maybe." She nodded entering the house. But she had a feeling finding out the truth of who started the fire would only get more difficult before the whole story saw the light of day.

Her body trembled as she thought about who they would discover was behind this.

Rory only hoped they would uncover the truth soon.

CHAPTER ELEVEN

ory

RORY STRETCHED and opened her eyes to a sliver of daylight shining through the yellow gingham curtains in her room.

Rubbing her eyes she breathed in the scent of cooked chicken.

She sat up in bed as she remembered Mrs. O'Toole had arrived last evening.

Rory was quite happy that the cook Gabe hired arrived yesterday.

She had shown the older lady the guesthouse and she seemed happy with the arrangement. She had hurried to clean it before she arrived so their cook would feel right at home.

It was strange to have someone to cook for them. Rory

felt guilty for not cooking for her and Gabe, but admitted it was a blessing she wasn't about to turn down.

Turning to look at the nightstand her gaze fell on her mother's diary. She had started reading the first journal entry last night. So far, she had learned about her mother's years in college and gained more insight into her mother's family.

As she read the journal, her mother wrote about her alcoholic father and how he'd hurt her mother — Keeva Murphy — and his five daughters over and over again. Rory knew that her mother was younger than Florrie, Fawn and Merrie, but she had never heard much about her mom — Delanie's — oldest sister Aunt Mallory. Her mom called her Mal.

From her mother's perspective Aunt Mal had taken a lot of abuse from Cedric Murphy - her grandfather - every time he was in one of his alcoholic stupors.

She wrote that her grandfather had died when her mother had started college. All five sisters had all come to his funeral to support her grandmother but she'd written that they were all better off without him in their lives.

Rory thought it was so sad that her grandfather's addiction to alcohol had caused him to be abusive to the family he loved.

After grandfather died her mother wrote that something must have snapped in her sister Mal because she never contacted them anymore.

She tried to call her oldest sister and wrote that she often asked her to go for coffee but Mal always pushed her away.

Her mom was sad about that but did her best to keep

in touch with her other three sisters and to make friends at college so she wouldn't be so lonely.

Last night Rory had just got to the part where her mom graduated college and got a job working as a writer for a popular magazine.

For Rory the story was just getting interesting because her mother had wrote that she just met her husband-to-be, Edward Shepard — Rory's Dad. She hadn't read anything after that because Razelle texted.

"How's married life?"

"Um, good."

"But not great? Come on Rory, I need more."

"Well Gabe treats me well. But every time I think we're getting closer, he pulls away."

"I bet he's scared of what being with you does to him."

"You think so?"

"I'd bet my last dollar on it."

"Hmm. I'm not sure."

"Has he kissed you yet... I mean a real kiss?"

"Yes."

"Then he's terrified. Which explains why he pulls away whenever he feels he's getting too close to you."

"What do I do?

"Keep showing Gabe that you love him and keep getting under his skin. One day he'll realize he can't let you go."

"I hope so. Thanks Raz I needed to hear that today."

"That's what friends are for. See you later."

Rory pondered her friend's words.

The truth was she wasn't sure if Raz was right about Gabe. But she was looking forward to spending more time with her husband.

Hearing her dogs whining outside her bedroom, Rory got up and opened her door.

Her eyes widened with surprise to see Gabe standing there.

Rory nervously tucked a hair behind her head. "Good morning, Gabe." His eyes lowered to take in her pajamas.

She looked down at the large Seahawk's t-shirt and a pair of cotton shorts, which were her normal nightwear. Heat stained her cheeks as she realized she must look like a rumpled mess. "Sorry I'll change my clothes in a minute."

"Don't change on my account. I think you look beautiful rumpled. I was just admiring the view." Gabe blue eyes darkened and glittered with appreciation for a moment before he spoke again. "Mrs. O'Toole wanted you to know lunch will be ready soon."

He walked away whistling.

Rory closed the door leaning her head against it. *He thought she looked beautiful rumpled and was admiring the view?* A small tugged her lips upwards. She couldn't hold back a smile as she slipped on a pair of jeans and her favorite pink sweater.

Brushing out her blonde hair she added some mascara to make her violet eyes look bigger and some light pink lip-gloss to her lips.

Maybe today would be the day she would begin to get under Gabe's skin as Raz put it.

She opened her door and walked toward the dining room, her dogs at her side.

"Mocha and Latte lie down." Her dogs lay down in the corner while she joined Gabe at the table. He pulled out a chair for her and sat down in Grand's old spot at the head of the table.

A salad had already been placed on the table along with plates and water glasses.

"You sitting in that chair brings back fond memories of your great-grandfather drinking his coffee and reading his newspaper." A wave of nostalgia hit her as she remembered. "I really miss him."

"I do too." Gabe put his hand on top of hers squeezing it for a moment. "But we can make our own memories in this place."

Rory peered at him for a moment and wondered if he really meant it. When he talked about them making memories together it sounded like a long-term marriage not just a fake marriage with a time limit. "Yes, of course we will."

At that moment Mrs. O'Toole walked into the dining room and Rory sighed at the interruption.

Her grey hair was tied up in braided coronet that circled her head from ear to ear. A long red apron covered the jeans and western styled shirt she wore.

Their cook wore a smile that only added sweetness to her plump cheeks. With a smile, she set down a pan of chicken casserole on the hot plate in the middle of the table. "Here you go. Lunch is served. Enjoy."

"Thank you Mrs. O'Toole. This looks delicious. Will you be joining us?" Rory asked looking her way.

"No my dear. I will be preparing for the next meal and adding some healthy snack trays to your refrigerator. You two enjoy." With a nod their cook walked back to the kitchen.

"I don't think I've had delicious food like this for a long time." Gabe savored each bite.

"Me either. This is wonderful. Gabe my taste-buds thank you for bringing Mrs. O'Toole to us." Rory savored each bite.

He grinned. "You're welcome."

They didn't talk much during the meal it was so delicious.

As soon as they finished eating Gabe spoke. "Did you get a chance to look through the bags of dried sea plants that arrived yesterday?"

"Yes. They look really good. I already sent an email to Maria thanking her and her family for hand harvesting these sea plants. She replied back saying her family was grateful for this work and let me know they got the payment we sent." She sighed happily.

"Maria told me her parents were so happy for the income because now her brothers and little sisters would be able to go to school to make something of themselves. I was encouraged by her email." Rory took a sip of water looking at Gabe thoughtfully.

"You've really helped Maria and her family. You've done something wonderful. Not that I'm surprised. You have always been a very compassionate and thoughtful woman." Gabe reached over and held her hand rubbing his thumb along the top of her hand.

Rory noticed he was doing that a lot more lately. Touching her back, holding her hand or kissing her forehead. Warmth spread from her toes upwards as memories surfaced of the many ways Gabe treated her with gentleness.

He was only being kind and gentle with her. She had convinced herself he didn't mean anything more by it.

Biting her lip, she reminded herself not to hope for more between them. That way her hopes wouldn't be dashed.

Forcing a smile she talked about her plans for later that day. "I'm excited to mix the next batch of the skin care formula today." Rory had a list as long as her arm of things to do.

"You have an eager waiting list?"

She thought of the long list of names on her computer. "Yes. Over a hundred women eagerly waiting their skin care creams. I'll need to bring the boxes with me for the Saturday's Market so people can get what they ordered." Rory realized she would need to work fast to get this all done in time.

"We can do that. We'll need to leave in a couple days so that we're in Seattle for Friday for the day with my family and the benefit gala. Then it shouldn't be a problem to stop by to deliver your products the next day." Gabe tapped his chin thoughtfully. "I wonder if you'll need extra help before long?"

"Maybe at some point. I'm okay for right now." Rory had always been able to handle multi-tasking but she wondered if this time she had bitten off more than she could chew. "Fingers crossed that I will have this finished in two days."

"You'll be able to do get it done no problem. But before we both get to work I thought we could walk to the construction site. I want to show you around." Gabe blue eyes held hers as he waited for her answer.

Rory nodded and smiled unable to resist spending time with him. "That would be fun. I'd love that."

It seemed Gabe was beginning to like spending time with her.

She only hoped it would continue.

❦

"THIS IS where we'll build the Health Spa. It'll be like an extension to the large Hotel." Gabe put his hand on the small of her back as they walked together following the stakes with red flags that were in the ground.

Gabe wanted to show Rory the Resort area that was now under construction.

He couldn't explain this longing he had for Rory to see and hopefully appreciate the long-time dream he had that was just now beginning to see the light of day.

Around them were at least a dozen men and women wearing hard hats all of who were busy measuring wood and hammering together the framed building of the small hotel.

"Mocha and Latte." Rory called her dogs and they ran to her quickly.

Loud machinery and hammering along with chatter surrounded them, and the dogs quivered a little at the sound.

"The dogs are afraid. There's more activity here this month than Walker's Island has seen in a year. I think it's throwing them off their game a little." Rory patted their heads and they seemed to calm a little.

Gabe reached down to pat their heads knowing her

dogs were unsure of him still. "You're good with them. They seem to shy away from me."

"They just need time to get used to you Gabe. Keep petting them and playing with them. They'll warm up to you." Rory reassured him.

He really wanted to get to know her dogs better. The furry creatures had become her friends over the last few years and Gabe hoped to grow to love them like she did.

He grimaced. "I hope so Rory. I haven't had a dog since I was in grade school. I might need a little practice."

"No worries. Dogs are patient. They must be or why else would they be called a man's best friend?" She giggled at him.

"You got me there." Gabe grinned and winked at her.

He loved it when they bantered good-naturedly back and forth. It reminded him of their summers together. It was great that they could return so quickly to the friendship they had back then.

An uncomfortable twinge formed in his belly. He couldn't deny that now that he'd been with Rory for a couple of weeks he was beginning to want a lot more than friendship.

How was he going to deal with that?

Rory sighed. "I'm sorry I interrupted you with my talk of dogs. Please go on."

Gabe chuckled. "I don't mind."

They walked a little further and he began to point out how the Resort and Health Spa would be connected and the benefits for all the people who stayed here.

"I can hear the passion in your voice." She expelled a happy sigh. "Now that you've explained where all these buildings will be located I can see it in my mind's eye. It looks great. Gabe I'm so excited for you. This resort and health spa will be amazing."

"I hope so but I think the Health Spa will be missing something unless you contribute."

"What?" Rory turned to him, her eyes widening at the thought. "In what way could I possibly add anything that you don't already have?"

"Your organic skincare products of course." Gabe chuckled shaking his head.

He pulled her close and kissed her forehead the rumble of laughter still in his chest. "Rory so far you've only offered your skin care products at the local farmer's markets am I right?"

"Well yes. I mean I started making those creams to help my aunts. But then folks at the Paradise Lake farmer's market became interested in the sea plant based formula so I started to make more. But I never thought it would go further than that." Rory looked at him her eyes wide. "I guess I'm just surprised that you would add my simple skin creams to your luxury health spa.

"You my darling wife have created an organic skin care line that people are clamoring for and it seems you're the only one who doesn't know it." Gabe shook his head still grinning.

Rory was one-of-a-kind.

Naively she only thought that people around their small town would be the only folks interested in the skin creams she had to offer.

But he knew better.

He'd seen people from one end of the country to the

other and he knew there would be many more who would love the products she formulated.

"Maybe." Her brow puckered looking doubtful. "But I have to admit I'm surprised and amazed that you would add my products to your Health Spa that caters to people who insist on luxury and pampering."

"You have created something that many ladies will consider a luxury and they will feel pampered once they try it." He spoke from a confidence born of experience.

She shrugged and grinned at him. "If you think it's a good idea then I'd be very pleased to add my products."

"I know this might feel overwhelming, but this will be good for you as well as the Health Spa." He tugged her hand and pulled her beside him. "Come a little closer and I'll explain the layout of the place."

He invited her to imagine with him. "In the front will be the reception area with a nice bright and sunny feel to it. Behind that will be the different areas like a salt-scrub bar to exfoliate your skin, two steam rooms and two sauna rooms. And of course lounge chairs both outside and inside where people can sit and read in between steam sessions. Right next door will be a tearoom for people to enjoy after they've been through the spa. So what do you think?"

Gabe gaze looked to his wife, feeling happiness bubble inside him as he imagined how it would look when it was finished.

Rory giggled softly. "That's great you are so eager for this project to become reality. I believe this will be the best health spa around. You've thought of everything. And all the people that come to the Island will realize how well you've planned this. They'll love it."

"I think so too. As soon as they have the small hotel framed in they are going to begin over here with the Health Spa. I can hardly wait for them to start." He looked around feeling satisfied with the progress that was being made on this project.

He walked beside Rory enjoying her closeness.

"You're like a kid on Christmas morning." Her violet eyes danced.

"I have to admit I am. I've dreamed about doing something like this ever since I was in middle school and Grand started bringing me to the Island in the summer." Gabe looked toward the beach as memories flooded him.

"A Hotel and Resort to help people find joy again was only the beginning. The fuller picture came later. After my Dad passed away I thought about the idea for the Health Spa and realized this resort wouldn't be complete without it. People need a way to get rid of stress, find peace, be refreshed and get a new perspective for their lives. If my Dad would've had a similar type of support I'm convinced he would still be alive today. But that was not to be."

"I'm sorry Gabe. You lost your Dad far too young." Rory eyes held a shine of tears. "I remember the summer that your Dad died, because you didn't come to the Island. Your great-grandfather told my aunts what happened. I remember saying a prayer for you and hoping you would return the next summer. And you did but you were still going through so much pain."

"Those were very difficult years." Gabe tucked her

hand in his as they walked. "You helped me get through them."

She squeezed his hand. He knew she was trying to offer what comfort she could.

"I helped you? What did I do?" Looking back Rory thought she'd only been a pest. Always asking Gabe questions and following him around like a puppy.

Gabe grinned. "You kept talking to me and asking me questions. You didn't let me wallow in my own sorrow. Because you were there I needed to talk and that really helped heal my heartache."

"I didn't realize that. I'm glad if I was able to help even a little."

They had reached the beach where they used to spend so much time together. Mocha and Latte ran along the water's edge chasing each other. In that moment Gabe felt closer to Rory than ever before.

"Thanks for telling me. It helps me understand a little more about your passion behind building the resort and health spa." Rory looked over at him.

He said, "I'm not the only one who lost a parent, Rory. You lost both of your parents and at such a tender age. I still remember when you came to the Island scared and shaking."

"Yes. I was terrified. I had just lost both my parents and in my child-like mind, I couldn't understand why they abandoned me." Rory blinked trying to force the tears to go away. "But then you came along. You helped me not be so scared anymore."

Gabe stopped her suddenly.

He looked up at the tree pointing his finger to the spot

they'd carved their names. "When I first saw you, you were six years old and so scared you were shaking. Do you remember what I told you?"

Rory smiled, the memory as fresh now as it was back then. "You told me that this tree was a special. It had roots that went down the deepest of all the trees on the Island. You said if we both carved our names together into the tree the Island would remember us and we would build deep roots here and be safe. I believed you."

"Did you feel safer?"

"I did but I think it was because you were there that made me feel safe. Somewhere in my little girls heart I knew I could trust you." Rory reached up and traced a finger along each of their names. "And you proved that again when you promised you would marry me if I was still scared when I grew up."

"And here we are." Gabe focused his gaze on Rory thinking how lucky he was.

"Yes, here we are years later."

"And we still have another fear to tackle — or at least the person who is causing it." He tucked her blond hair behind her ears, worry for Rory's safety niggling at him. That someone was out there waiting to hurt his wife was one of his worst fears.

"But we will." She lowered her hand from the tree and looked at him. "Besides that's not the only kind of fears that are difficult. Sometimes the biggest fear of all is being willing to take a risk and let ourselves get close to someone else."

Without thinking Gabe took a step closer to her. "Rory

you're the best thing that's ever happened to me." He leaned his head down his forehead touching hers.

"Maybe we should take that risk right now." He looked at Rory and seeing a shine in her violet eyes he put his arms around her waist and pulled her close. Leaning down he pressed his lips against her sweet fullness loving the feel of her in his arms.

Shaping his lips to hers, he pressed in deeper. He couldn't get enough of her sweetness.

Something brushed against his arm and he tried to shove it away. Just as quickly, it returned again.

He pulled back from Rory and saw Mocha and Latte standing on their hind legs pressing their large paws against him.

Rory giggled. "They want to play with you."

Gabe shook his head with a grin. "Right now?"

He looked at Rory and grabbed her hand. "I was enjoying the best kiss I've ever had and I'm bothered by dogs who want to play. Next time we're going to go somewhere where there will be no interruptions."

Rory kissed his cheek quickly before turning to Latte and Mocha who waited patiently.

"But for now we can play with the dogs." Rory chased them along the beach and threw a stick to each dog.

Gabe stared after Rory the corners of his mouth upturned.

There would never be a dull moment with Rory as his wife but he wouldn't want it any other way.

CHAPTER TWELVE

ory

RORY SAT beside Eliza Stevenson in the steam room of Seattle's Beauty Spa her head leaning back against the wood.

On her other side were Elle, Bella and Catherine Stevenson.

She was trying desperately to relax but the tense morning she'd had with Gabe was making it impossible.

They had been so close last night as they walked on the beach, but he had already started to pull away from her this morning.

When she entered the kitchen to get a cup of coffee, he'd said a quick good morning and then made a beeline to his office to do some work.

Afterwards when it had been time for her to leave,

Gabe had simply said his driver would take her to the Health Spa.

Her husband had given her a forced smile and sent her on her way.

Rory sighed. Maybe all she needed to do was talk to him. Then everything between them would be good again.

It had felt so good that they were growing closer. She didn't want to lose what they had.

Someone patted her knee interrupting her reverie.

"I'm sorry, what's that?"

"I said this is perfect. I feel like my pores are getting the cleaning they've deserved for a long time." Eliza whispered beside her. "What about you my dear? How are you feeling sitting here surrounded by all this heat and steam?"

Rory grimaced and leaned over to Eliza. "This is my first time trying this. But I think I could get used to it. My skin feels so soft and moist."

Eliza chuckled softly. "Well, we'll need to do this again then. What do you think Bella and Elle?"

"I'm definitely coming back. This is perfect. It's so nice to have Jack at home taking care of our son." Bella sighed contentedly.

"I could get used to this too. With baby number two on the way I would love some time away being pampered like this." Elle looked over at Rory. "You might feel the same way Rory once you have your first baby."

Heat flew up to her cheeks at Elle's words.

"You might be right." She was already hot from the steam so she hoped they wouldn't see that Elle's words flustered her. Staying married for real with Gabe and having babies was something she held onto only in her dreams.

Gabe and her were in a marriage-of-convenience but Elle didn't know that.

If someone would've asked her yesterday she would have said if Gabe's kisses were any indication there was hope their fake marriage would become a real after all.

She had even dreamed of his kisses last night and woke up feeling happy that Gabe was opening up to her.

This morning however there was a chill in the air as far as Gabe was concerned. It seemed all the closeness they'd been building toward melted.

"It's too early for that. They're just married. Let them get used to each other first before you bring babies into the picture." Catherine spoke from her place on the side of the steam room. "But that being said you know Granddad and I and your mom are more than happy to welcome as many grand babies into the Stevenson family as you want to give us."

"I'll remember that." Rory was sure her cheeks were flaming red by now. All their talk of babies was only making her more flustered.

She was relieved when the soft buzzing of a timer went off signalling their time was up in the steam room.

They each took a light shower and then applied cold towels to their bodies and met in the lounge room. They were going to have facials, manicures and pedicures.

Rory was once more seated beside Gabe's mom. Each of them had a female therapist who gave them a facial treatment. The cleansing cream felt wonderful on Rory's skin. After that treatment was done they each put cold slices of cucumber on their eyes and rested with their heads back on the lounge chairs.

"So tell me Rory, what's it like living in Gabe's great-grandfather's Hunting Lodge? It must be somewhat of a change from living in the cottage." Eliza spoke softly, her voice kind and soothing.

"It's been good. Gabe has shown me around the large place and I'm starting to get used to it. It's especially helpful now that your son hired Mrs. O'Toole as our cook."

"That's so good that you have her to help you. Gabe has been telling me how much he admires you." Eliza commented.

"Really he said that?" She was surprised. Gabe didn't always say what he was feeling and it was nice to hear that her husband had said nice things about her to his own mom.

"Oh yes, whenever I talk to Gabe lately he's mentions little details of what you're doing. I can tell by his tone of voice that you are very special to him."

If only that were really true. Even with Gabe's recent toe curling kisses she knew their agreement.

This was a marriage based on convenience not love. Gabe had made that quite clear right from the start. But she couldn't help but be drawn to the warm and cozy picture Eliza painted of a couple that loved each other.

Rory wished it could be true for them.

"He has spoken of your talent for writing and that you've written quite a few romance novels." Eliza leaned over to whisper. "I've already read two of your romance novels and I quite like them."

"Thank you for saying that. I'm happy you've enjoyed reading them." Rory couldn't help but smile. She was thrilled her own mother-in-law liked the books she'd written. "My aunts tell me they like my books too but it feels extra-special to hear it from you."

"You're sweet Rory just like Gabe said. My son also told me that when you went to Argentina on your honeymoon you helped to get a woman away from a man who was using her in his human-trafficking schemes."

"Well it was Gabe's private investigator who discovered the man's background and had charges laid against him. But yes Gabe and I had Maria as a maid in our room at the resort and so it was so good when she was finally freed from forced slavery to that man."

Eliza expelled a breath sighing heavily. "I'm so glad you were there." Her mother-in-law's heartfelt compassion reminded her that Gabe's mom had also been rescued from a terrible situation. Rory appreciated the new and unexpected closeness that was developing between them born of shared experiences and compassion for others.

"Gabe tells me you also have contracted your work for harvesting sea plants to their family." Her mother-in-law shifted in her chair to see her better.

"Yes. Maria says it's been very helpful for her family. But I'm not the only one who has helped Maria, Gabe was also very helpful in all of this. He too was convinced of Maria's innocence and wanted to do what he could to help her. Gabe is the most kind and generous man I've ever known."

Eliza chuckled softly. "He is. Gabe's been like that all his life. He's always done whatever he could to protect and help the innocent. And even more so after his father passed away." Gabe's mom's voice shook as she told the story.

"He would come to Walker's Island and do what he could to protect the animals and people. One time there was a boat that got lost in a storm and ended up on the shore of the Island. It was Gabe who found them almost drowned on the beach and he helped the man and woman get to the Lodge. Grand told me later that Gabe was the one that cared for them, helping them to heal after their near drowning experience." Rory could hear the pride and a glow of love in Eliza's voice as she spoke of her son.

"Gabe was quite shaken up by the incident as I recall. He told me later it reminded him of what happened in middle school." Eliza sighed heavily before she continued.

"Gabe hung around with his good friend Billy quite a lot during those years. But one year Billy was bullied into a dare by the popular boys in school. They wanted Billy to dive off a cliff into the rushing river below. None of them had ever dived there before but Billy had always wanted to be noticed by the popular guys so he went along with it. Gabe told him not to do it. But Billy dived into those icy waters anyway and died on impact."

"I didn't know that. I'm so sorry."

"It was hard on him. After Gabe's Dad and Billy both passed away, those years were a really difficult time in his life."

"What happened to Billy's family?"

"Gabe went to their house after the accident but Billy's parents didn't want to see him. So, he tried to talk to

Billy's younger brother Danny. At first Danny didn't want anything to do with him.

He shied away from Gabe and only spoke when asked a direct question. In fact Danny was mean to him at first, saying he was convinced Gabe was going to abandon him and leave him just like everyone else did. But Gabe persisted and eventually he and Danny became good friends playing basketball and other sports together. Eventually, Billy's parents came around and realized that Gabe was a good guy and a real friend to their son."

A knot formed in her belly. Rory realized how much like Danny she was. She had been innocent and naive, in need of someone to care for her.

Small incidents drifted to the top of her mind like the brushstrokes of a painting coming together. Gabe had always rescued the innocent. It's what he did throughout their childhood together and now since he came back to the Island. He'd married her to save her from the person who was trying to harm her.

"Is Gabe still friends with Danny today?" The knot in Rory's belly grew bigger, afraid of the answer.

"They're not as close as they once were."

"Maybe Gabe got tired of Danny's prickly and fearful ways and lost interest in their friendship."

"As Gabe got into High School he got busier, but they still continued to play basketball once a week. When Gabe started college they drifted apart each busy with their own lives. They have a passing friendship, but both Gabe and Danny have other friends now and have moved on with their own families."

A strange chill swept down Rory's arms settling in her

stomach. She made every effort to hide her misery from Gabe's mom.

All of her husband's wonderful and encouraging words to her had been only to make Rory feel better about herself. But, the truth was Gabe hadn't really accepted her as she was. Not really.

To him she was a naive and innocent Island girl who was helpless and needed to be rescued.

Gabe didn't really believe she was the best thing that had happened to him. Just like Billy's younger brother whom he had rescued, Gabe would one day abandon her too.

Memories of what she'd read last night in her mother's diary came back to haunt her. *Edward and I have been married for three years now. There's still no child. I'm so sad about that. My biggest fear though, is that my husband's attention has started to drift elsewhere. I saw lipstick on the corner of his shirt when I did the laundry yesterday. And he's not at home as much as he once was. I am very afraid he's abandoned me for someone else.*

Her own father had drifted away from her mom discarding her as not important. Rory's fears came back. She was convinced Gabe's interest would wander and his feelings for her would fade. Perhaps they already had.

A deadness spread from Rory's heart down to the rest of her body. She was numb inside. It was like all her hopes and dreams for anything more between her and Gabe had been tossed aside.

Somehow she made it through the rest of their time at the spa and did her best to enjoy the light meal and tea they had at their Catherine's favorite tea place.

"Now we will go shopping for tonight." Eliza called for her driver to pick them up to take them to her choice of designer clothing stores. "We'll stop here please Henry. I'll text you when we've finished shopping."

"I'll be waiting, Mrs. Stevenson."

They walked along the boulevard and began shopping at a store that had quite a collection of *Oscar De La Renta* clothing. Rory followed Eliza down the aisle where the evening wear was located. Rory's jaw hung down as she looked at the prices. One dress cost two months wages.

While Bella and Elle looked in the other aisle, a woman who worked there came to help them.

"We're looking for a beautiful evening gown for my daughter-in-law. Could you show us some ideas of what you think would look good on her?" Eliza smiled at the associate and nodded at Rory.

"Of course. Follow me to the very special dresses. There are a few there I think will be beautiful on her." The lady had a slight French accent and seemed to glide across the store as she walked.

Rory followed Eliza and the woman from the store, feeling a little intimidated by all the luxury that surrounded her. She'd never been in these high-end stores in her life. Nor had she worn designer clothing.

Being here in this store together with Gabe's mom, Grandmom and her two sister-in-laws, made her realize how far apart their worlds really were.

The lady from the store had a few dresses draped over her arm when she returned, and at Eliza's nod Rory was shown into a spacious dressing room.

Stepping outside the dressing room with each new

dress she tried on Rory watched her mother-in-law's expression for signs of approval. It wasn't until the last one that Eliza nodded. "That deep purple color looks beautiful on you Rory. The *Venus* off-the-shoulder tulle is a beautiful look on you and it hugs your slim figure perfectly. What do you think Rory?"

"I've never worn anything so beautiful. I do love it."

"Perfect. We'll take it." Eliza Stevenson spoke decisively to the associate who was eagerly waiting by the time Rory slipped out of the dress and into her walking clothes.

Before long everyone had bought their evening dresses and the accessories they needed. Bella and Elle also helped Rory find some wonderful designer shirts and pants in colors that enhanced her natural creamy complexion.

As soon as Eliza's driver picked them up, they leaned their heads back against the seats very tired from their full day.

Rory was happy when she got back to Gabe's condo. As she walked through the door all was quiet.

Gabe wasn't back yet from wherever he'd gone to. It looked like any conversation would need to wait until tonight.

"Yes I have a few conferences coming up where I'll be speaking. All my trainings and conferences schedule you can find on my website..." Gabe spoke to a few people who had seen his recent interview on the Winny O show.

He was about to share more details when his gaze was

captivated by a woman looking beautiful in a deep purple gown standing in the middle of the room.

Rory was a beautiful vision.

"Sorry everyone I need to go. There's someone I need to talk to." Gabe swallowed as he walked toward his wife.

He had returned to the condo only a few minutes before they needed to leave.

Gabe had spent the afternoon catching up with his brothers. Then as his driver drove them to the benefit gala he had been so busy prepping for his speech that he'd all but forgot about his wife.

However the biggest reason he'd kept busy was because fear gripped him at how quickly they were becoming close to each other. It scared him.

On some level, the intimacy that had begun with Rory during their week in Argentina had brought his deep-seated fears to the surface.

An increased level of awareness flooded him that his new wife was chipping away at the walls he had carefully placed around his heart.

Tonight Gabe knew he needed to try to do what he could to fix things with Rory.

"You look stunningly beautiful. Sorry I got caught up in yet another conversation and left you alone." He walked up to her and kissed her cheek.

Large violet eyes widened as her gaze lifted to his uncertainty in her gaze.

"I understand. A lot of people want to talk with you." Her forced smile and her cool tone of voice convinced him she didn't really understand at all.

"Rory, can we talk later?"

"Sure." Tucking her hand under his arm he led her toward a table near the stage where most of his family was seated with their hosts Cyrus and Anna Noble.

"Rory it's so wonderful you're here." Eliza stood and kissed her on the cheek. "You remember Cyrus and Anna from your wedding?"

Rory held out her hand as she greeted them. "Yes of course. It's nice to see you again."

His wife smiled nodding at his grandparents, mother and brothers and their wives. Gabe could tell she was nervous and he lightly squeezed her hand to reassure her.

They ate their meal together bantering back and forth. Gabe sensed that Rory wasn't her usual self tonight. They would need to talk later.

Soon Cyrus made his way onto the stage. "We're here because we care about what goes on in our neighborhoods, our state and our nation. We all want to give back. Many of us have had the privilege of aiding many causes like helping orphans and aiding the fight against poverty. However tonight's gala, the donations will be to help victims of human trafficking. Someone who has recently been in this fight is here to share with you his story. Please welcome Gabe Stevenson."

"Thank you Cyrus." Gabe shook his hand and stood behind the microphone. "You're here because you want to end human trafficking. From recent experience, I can tell you it's a battle worth fighting."

He paused and looked over the large crowd gathered. Everyone was listening with rapt attention and it inspired him tell his story. "Here's my story of the battle we just fought against this horrible crime. My wife and I recently went on our honeymoon to a port town in Argentina. We thought we were going to experience an exciting adventure, but it turned out to be much more than that."

"My kind and compassionate wife, saw that our maid Maria was fearful every time she would come to our room. One day Rory observed a man getting very angry with Maria and she could tell our maid was really scared. When my wife asked her what was wrong, our maid didn't want to say anything, but my wife pressed her for answers. Maria finally told her she couldn't say anything because if she did the man would hurt her family."

Gabe shook his head and paused looking over the crowded room. "Most of us have not been in that position where we are forced to do something because if we don't someone will harm our family. But Maria was and because my wife persisted in getting answers we found out the man's name."

"When the police looked up his records they discovered that not only was he involved in human trafficking, but also in drug smuggling and other illegal activities. Now this man is behind bars and Maria is safe with her family once again. Because you have given to this important cause many more people like Maria will be set free to return home to their families once again."

Gabe paused letting the importance of his words sink in. "Cyrus and Anna Noble our hosts tonight have chosen to give tonight's proceeds to the *Stevenson BeSafe Foundation* which includes the Safe House where we've been able to help many people who have been forced into slavery against their will. Our mission is to free them and help them get healthy and back into society."

"My mom was a victim of human trafficking years ago and my Dad helped rescue her. My father has since passed away but like my mom always tells us she imagines her husband looking down from heaven with a smile lighting his face tonight telling us, you've done well. And you have. Thank you for joining with us in supporting this cause."

Loud clapping began and people stood to their feet.

Gabe stepped off the stage and walked toward his family's table. People shook his hand on the way back telling him that his words helped them have greater understanding and compassion towards victims of human trafficking.

It seemed to have struck a chord with people at tonight's benefit and for that he was grateful.

"You did well son." Granddad thumped his elaborately carved wooden cane at his side.

"You made me tear up, Gabriel." Grandmom pulled out a tissue from her purse and dabbed at the corner of her eyes. Gabe reached down to kiss her cheek.

"Son, you always make me proud." His mom hugged him and kissed his cheek.

His brothers gave him good-natured fist bumps as he passed them walking toward his own seat at the table.

He sat down beside Rory and looking at her whispered. "Well?"

Gabe couldn't believe he was more nervous to hear his wife's response than he was to speak in front of a roomful of people.

"You did really well Gabe. Your words touched a lot of people. I'm very proud of you." Her violet eyes misted with tears as she spoke softly.

"Thank you. I needed to hear those words from you most of all." Gabe whispered in her ear pleased when a blush stained her cheeks.

In spite of the warmth that flooded him at his wife's encouraging words, Gabe's regret of the evening was that he wasn't on the receiving end of Rory's beautiful smile.

He needed to figure out how to bring it back.

"IF YOU'LL EXCUSE me I need to go to the little girls room." Rory whispered to Gabe. He was in between conversations with one of his brothers.

"Of course."

Rory walked into the washroom glad that it was quiet. Thoughts swirled round and round in her head of Gabe's kind words about her when he talked tonight. But, just as quickly her thoughts returned to his Mom's words of how her son protected the naïve and innocent.

Being here tonight with all these well-dressed society people Rory had an even greater awareness of how unsophisticated she really was.

Returning to wash her hands she sighed looking forward to the end of this evening. Maybe she was just tired and overthinking things?

Without warning the door opened and a woman walked into the washroom. Rory caught a glimpse of low cut purple evening gown with a slit that was cut high up to the top of her thighs.

Without an introduction the woman spoke. "You came

here tonight with Gabe Stevenson." Her green eyes flashed, waiting for an answer.

"Yes. I'm his wife." Rory was about to introduce herself but the woman in front of her continued talking almost without taking a breath.

"I'd heard that Gabe married but didn't think he'd actually do it." There was unfriendliness to her tone that made Rory wary. "You're certainly not model material, which makes me wonder what he saw in you. Where are you from?"

"I grew up with my three aunts on Walker's Island." This conversation was beginning to feel more like an interrogation than a conversation. Rory continued to grow more uncomfortable with every passing minute.

"Ah yes. I've heard about you from friends. They told me Gabe married a poor little Island girl with no class or culture." She shook her head from side to side, red hair swaying with every movement. "Well you won't stay married to Gabe for long. He needs a woman who will help him get to the top, not drag him down. Gabe needs a woman with a lot more to offer than someone like you could possibly give him. Don't worry, when he finishes with you I'll be there waiting."

Rory stiffened at the insults hurled at her. "What did you say your name was?"

She glided toward the door opening it and turning suddenly before she left.

"Maddie Winslow."

The door closed with a soft ticking sound like the sound of a clock that was running out of time. The sound served as a reminder that her time as Gabe's wife was coming to an end.

Rory tried to ignore the inkling of doubt that sat heavy in the pit of her belly.

The worst part was Maddie Winslow was right.

She lacked all the culture and sophistication Gabe needed in a wife. She didn't have charm or the model-like beauty that was necessary to a man as important as her husband.

Her brows puckered in worry and she wondered how long it take before Gabe realized it too.

CHAPTER THIRTEEN

abe

A PERSISTENT BUZZING jerked Gabe awake.

Fumbling in the dark he reached across to his night-stand and grabbed his phone.

"Gabe here." He pushed himself up in bed and rubbed his eyes. Only family members and a few other important people had this private number.

"Morning Gabe. It's Max Harrison."

Bracing himself he realized there could only be a few reasons Max was calling this morning and none of them good. "What's up?"

"There's been another fire on Walker's Island."

"What! Where?" Gabe did his best to keep his voice calm but his heart raced with anxiety.

"Someone started a fire at the Health Spa location last night. Don't worry the workers caught it and put the fire out."

Gabe breathed a sigh of relief.

"But the damage is done and the frame constructed for the Health Spa has been destroyed." Max's cool detached voice helped calm the fear building in Gabe.

Without a doubt they needed to find the person responsible for causing these fires... fast. "Did any of the workers see who did it?" He had hired workers who came with great recommendations but had he misplaced his trust in one of them?

Was there a disgruntled worker who was expressing his anger through burning things down?

"I asked around. No one saw who set the fire. However I looked through yesterday's videos from the hidden security cameras you added to the Resort area. We found something. But we need both you and Rory to meet me at my office to view the video so we can get a better idea of who we're dealing with."

Max's office was downtown and Rory was still sleeping after a late night. He would need to wake her. It couldn't be helped.

"Of course. We'll be there in a few minutes." Gabe hung up the phone and stepped into the hallway staring at Rory's bedroom door.

He didn't like disturbing her sleep but this had to be done. With quiet movements he stepped inside her room and stopped. His wife looked so peaceful lying there beneath the fluffy white comforter.

Last night when they came home Rory had been

standoffish putting even more distance between them. They really needed to have that talk, but now wasn't the right time.

With gentle movements he shook her shoulder as he sat on the bed beside her. "Rory, I'm sorry but you need to wake up."

Before long she opened her eyes and sat up in bed. Seeing him nearby, her eyes widened.

"What's up?" She rubbed sleepy eyes trying to come awake.

Gabe thought he'd never seen anyone more adorable. He wanted to kiss her and if he were honest he wanted much more, but that would need to wait.

"Max phoned. Someone set fire to the Health Spa on the Island. We need to hurry to Max's office to look at some surveillance videos." Gabe could see Rory's eyes darting quickly down and then back up and knew that her thoughts were racing.

"My aunts are okay?"

"Yes and so are the workers. They put the fire out. But we need to go see this video footage. Maybe we'll be able to deal with this quickly." Gabe squeezed her hand and walked to the door before he turned.

"I'll be ready in fifteen minutes." Gabe nodded relieved that she understood him so well.

He hurried to shower and change and they met each other in the kitchen almost at the same time.

The drive to Max's office was quiet and a little tense.

Gabe parked the car and reaching over covered her hand with his. "It'll be okay. We'll figure out how to stop whoever is setting these fires and trying to scare us."

"Thanks. I know." Rory's eyes brimmed with unshed tears. He leaned over and kissed her cheek, then got out of the car hurrying to open her door and help her out.

As they dashed up the stairs to the office, Max was there to greet them.

"Good you're both here." Max looked over at his assistant. "Darien, could you bring some coffees and meet us in the media room?"

"Sure thing."

"Follow me and we'll take a look at these videos." Max led them into a large media room that held several computers. Three large computer monitors spanned the back wall and two of Max's assistants were working to get the video files up on the monitors.

Max indicated chairs for them to sit down and his assistant came into the room handing them each coffees.

"Okay looks like we're ready to go." Max took a sip of his coffee and pointed to the screens. "These videos are from different security cameras that are located near the Health Spa. Look at the monitor on the far left."

The security video showed a man at a distance walking up to the Health Spa. All Gabe could see was the hat he wore and his jeans and t-shirt. He used a lighter to set fire to a piece of cloth and threw it into the construction site.

"Hmm. There isn't much that I can identify in that video." Gabe looked at Rory.

"The images looked blurry to me too. Is there another video that has a closer shot?"

Max spoke to his assistant. "Yes. This next surveillance video will show the same man at a different angle." The video started playing. "Notice you can see his clothes in this shot."

"Looking up close now I see the t-shirt has the Portland State Vikings logo. But I still can't see his face."

"It looked like he turned to look toward the camera. Could we zoom in closer to this guy and run the video in slow motion?" Rory asked Max.

"Yes." Max's assistant ran the video again but in slow motion, zooming in for a better look.

"Stop right here." Rory stood to her feet her hands shaking. Gabe took the coffee cup from her hand and set it on the table.

"What is it? Who do you see?" Gabe put his arm around her shoulders and could feel her trembling.

On the monitor screen was a close-up of a male who looked to be around Rory's age. He was looking up and they could see his face.

"He looks like a younger version of my father." Rory's voice shook as she spoke.

"Do you have a cousin?"

Rory shook her head. "No. But lately I've been reading my mother's diary. My mom wrote that she was fairly certain my dad's interest had drifted to another woman. That was about three years into their marriage."

"When were you born?"

"They were married five years before I was born." Rory sucked in a breath staring at the video screen a hand over her mouth.

"You think he might be your half brother?" Gabe rubbed his hand on her back, trying to calm her fears.

"I do. He looks so much like my dad. He must be

related to me. And it seems like he's close to my age." Rory looked at Max and then Gabe. "This whole investigation just got a little more personal. I'd like to meet him and talk to him."

Max gave her a skeptical look. "We're still not sure that he's your half brother."

"No I'm not completely sure yet. However you did say that the DNA you found at the fire near the cottage was from a man named Ned Baxter?"

"Yes that's the name that came up in the data base." Max nodded his brows furrowed and hesitation in his voice.

"Well my dad's name was Edward Shepard. Do you think he might have chosen to go with the shortened form of Edward and call himself Ned? And maybe he decided to take his mother's last name?" Rory folded her arms across her chest.

Gabe nodded. "I think my wife might have solved the case Max."

"Maybe. But I still don't know if it's a good idea to talk to him. There's some reason he's been trying to scare you and attack things that are personal to you Rory." Max tried to reason with her.

"I know he probably has a personal vendetta against me. But I still want to talk to him before he's charged with anything. Can I do that?"

Max nodded. "Sure I'll get the information to the police in Oregon and let you know where you can find him."

"Okay. Thanks."

Gabe wasn't sure if Rory meeting her half brother was

a good idea. Especially since they were fairly certain he was responsible for setting the fires and scaring Rory and her aunts.

Still, if she really wanted to do this Gabe was determined he would be right by her side to protect her.

He couldn't let anyone else hurt his wife.

❧

RORY SAT beside Gabe fidgeting with her hands on her lap.

They were in one of the private meeting rooms at the police station in Portland, Oregon.

They had flown to the city right after Rory had delivered her skin care products to the clients at the market. The police hadn't taken very long at all to capture Ned Baxter. Max assured her that she could meet with him today.

"I can't believe we're here and I get to meet a half brother I never knew I had." Rory turned to Gabe still thinking the whole thing was unbelievable.

Gabe put his hand in hers. "Remember he is the same guy who set those fires and tried to harm you Rory."

"I know. But I still want to meet him and talk to him." Didn't Gabe understand? She never had any brothers or sisters growing up. Now she was finally meeting a half brother she never knew she had.

"Well you'll get your chance soon. But I'm not going anywhere. I will be right beside you to protect you." Gabe squeezed her hand lightly his blue eyes filled with the compassion and warmth.

"Thank you."

Without warning the door to the room opened and a guard brought a young man into the room. Handcuffs were on his wrists and a sullen expression was on his face.

He sat down in front of them and his eyes narrowed as he stared at Gabe and Rory.

She realized this would not be an easy conversation. "You are Ned Baxter?"

"Yes."

Obviously getting answers from him would be a little like finding a needle in a haystack. A prod here and a dab there.

"I'm Rory Shepard."

"I know who you are."

"You look so much like my father. I believe you might be my half brother." Nervously she pulled at her sleeves waiting for his response.

"Yeah so? Didn't want a brother messing up your life hey?"

Rory gave him a small smile. "Actually I very much want a brother in my life. I was by myself growing up and very lonely. I always dreamed of being part of a bigger family."

His eyes flickered with a little more interest but stayed silent.

"So I need to ask you an important question, Ned. Did you set both fires on Walker's Island — the one by the cottage and the other by the Heath Spa?"

"Yeah I did. I was just having a little fun."

Rory leaned closer feeling more confident after witnessing true emotion when she talked of family. "I think it was more than that. Please tell me the real reason you wanted to harm me and my aunts and Gabe here."

For a few moments he was silent and then like a waterspout being turned on his words gushed out. "I didn't want to harm you. I just wanted to scare you. You always had everything so easy. Dad was always home for you at least until the house fire. But me? I got the left-overs. He would visit once every six months maybe until finally he didn't show up at all. It's like my mom and me weren't worth his time anymore. No, instead my Dad had to go back to his princess Rory."

"So you just decided one day that you needed to get your revenge?"

Ned stared at her for a moment then said. "No, it was actually suggested to me by my mom's friend Mallory Murphy. She's your aunt I think? She hinted that I should scare you a little. Doing that might help me to feel better knowing that my half sister was getting a little of what she deserved."

"My Aunt Mal? Her name hasn't been mentioned by my three aunts for years." Rory was troubled by this new information. She decided to leave it there and ask her aunts later. "Please go on."

He took a breath and kept going. "I wanted to take away those things that you loved because you took away my Dad — the person I loved. Ironically even on the day he died he was celebrating your life — your birthday — not mine."

"I'm so sorry. I never knew." Tears brimmed over in Rory's eyes and slipped down her cheeks.

"It doesn't change the past."

"No but it could change the future."

"How do you figure? They have me here in handcuffs. I'll probably be locked away for a long time."

"If you promise you won't ever set fires again on Walker's Island I will ask the police to lessen the charges against you. I will ask them to lower it to a minor offense and community service."

Gabe turned to her his brows furrowed in worry. "What are you..."

Rory interrupted him. "This is the right thing to do. I feel it with everything in me."

He nodded slowly without saying a word.

"Why would you let me get off so easy?" Ned's eyes flickered with little bit of hope but the skepticism remained.

"For a couple of reasons. First you are my brother and my own flesh and blood. My dad would want me to do this. Second because I know what it's like to be treated like you're a second-class citizen. When I would go to take swimming lessons at the small town near the Island I was always teased by other kids. They called me the dumb Island girl who only had animal friends not people." Rory stopped realizing she probably shared too much.

Yet, she was encouraged to see Ned's eyes had lit up and the corners of his mouth turned up just a little.

"All right. I'll agree to your rules." Ned expelled a breath and continued. "And I'm sorry for setting those fires and for scaring you. I won't set anymore fires on Walker's Island."

"Thank you for that Ned." Rory stood up with Gabe at her side. "And once you've completed community service and proven you can be trusted maybe I can help you get setup with something you want to do."

Ned nodded a curious furrow now on his forehead. "That'd be all right."

Standing she nodded. "See you later Ned."

Rory talked more to the police asking them to lower the charges against Ned. After they finished at the police station they headed back to Gabe's plane.

As the plan took off, the sun was starting to set and Rory was tired but happy that there was a little more hope for her brother. Hopefully Ned would see this as a fresh start and begin to turn things around in his life.

Seated across from each other Gabe still eyed her, a lingering question in his gaze.

"You look like you have questions."

"I do. I realize Ned is your half brother but I just hope we're doing the right thing by letting him off so easy." Gabe rubbed the back of his neck concern in his eyes.

"I know it might not seem like the right thing but I have a gut feeling about this. I think Ned just needs another chance."

"If you would've died in one of those fires that your brother set you wouldn't have had a second chance." Gabe reasoned.

"No I wouldn't have. But it didn't go that far."

"I just want to protect you Rory but I can't if you make decisions that might not be wise."

"But we don't know that. It might be a great decision." Rory thought for a moment of her conversation with Gabe's mother. "Are you extra protective of me because of what happened years ago to your friend Billy?

"Who told you about Billy?"

"Your mother did when we were at the spa the other day. She mentioned how you tried to protect and save him. Your mom described him as too naive, trusting and simple about the ways of the world. Your mom said Billy just went along with those popular guys at school who were daring him to jump into those dangerous waters because he wanted to be popular and fit in too."

"Yes he was. I tried but he didn't listen to me. And he died."

"I'm sorry that happened to your friend Gabe, I really am."

"Yeah well sometimes those you really want to protect are the ones that end up dying.'

"Not always."

Gabe blue eyes were shadowed but he was silent.

"Your mom shared with me how innocent and trusting Billy was."

"Yeah he was."

Suddenly all of Rory's fears came back, that she wasn't good enough to be Gabe Stevenson's wife. What Maddie Winslow had said at the gala was true. She was a simple Island girl who didn't fit in.

"Sort of like me." Rory's voice wavered looking down at hands that shook on her lap for a moment before she looked at her husband again.

"You? How do you mean?" Gabe glanced up surprised. "I thought we were talking about my friend Billy."

"Yes but don't you see the similarity between your childhood friend and me?" She steadied herself suddenly needing to hear what her husband had to say.

Gabe looked taken aback. "That's the most ridiculous thing I've ever heard."

"Is it? Then tell me Gabe why did you marry someone like me — a lonely Island girl who is naive and simple and with no sophistication or culture? You could have married someone else who was more beautiful, elegant and had more knowledge of your world."

"My world? What does that mean?"

Rory expelled a breath she'd been holding. "You know like at the gala last night. People that have class who are wealthy and have a lot of knowledge and experience about how things should be done properly and with class."

Gabe shook his head and sent her a small smile. "Rory if truth be told many of those people are just real good at looking sophisticated on the outside when on the inside they are struggling."

"Well maybe, but my point is you could have married someone with more beauty and class, who wasn't naive like I was. So why didn't you marry a woman like that?"

"All the other women were superficial. You've always been honest and real about what you needed Rory. I've always liked that about you."

"And you wanted to rescue me from the whoever was setting the fires." Rory realized the part about her needing Gabe to protect her from the person setting the fires wasn't true anymore. They had found the guy responsible.

"Yes, I wanted to protect you." Gabe spoke quietly. "I still do Rory."

"Maybe but you still could have married someone who was better for you. Someone who understands how to do everything properly and be the wife of someone like you who has the influence and fame you have."

"I don't care about all that. I just wanted to do the right thing and be helpful to you."

"This may surprise you Gabe Stevenson. But I care. I have never wanted your pity. Just because I'm the Island girl who is poor and unsophisticated compared to the women friends you're used to dating doesn't mean that I need you to feel sorry for me." Rory wrapped her arms around herself rubbing her arms feeling a sudden chill.

"Rory, I didn't marry you because I felt sorry for you. You are my friend. I care about you and want to protect you."

She looked out the window of the airplane, swallowing back the frustration she felt. Her hands balled into a fist under the table.

"Well now it looks like I don't need protection anymore. Now that we know who is behind the fires you don't need to save me anymore."

"What are you saying Rory?"

"I'm saying maybe it's time we go back to our original agreement." Rory felt numb inside as she spoke. "We should decide that this is strictly a marriage-in-name-only and leave all emotions out of it."

"Is that really what you want Rory?" His voice held a chill, cool and detached.

"I think we would have less arguments that way. So yes, I think it would be better." The walls were up around her heart and she couldn't take any more pain or heartache. Something had shifted in her when Maddie had told her she wasn't good enough for Gabe.

She realized it really was true.

She would never fit into Gabe's world.

Her husband looked at her for a full minute before he spoke. His tone was crisp and detached. "If that's what you want Rory."

A sudden sadness swept over her. She didn't want it to be like this but she didn't know what else to do.

Her mind flooded with chaos, confusion and anger.

Tight knots of fear coiled in her belly at the thought of being abandoned again. She'd experienced the pain of that once already and was scared it would happen again.

She desperately wanted her husband to love her.

But that was not to be.

CHAPTER FOURTEEN

abe

SWEAT DRIPPED down his brow as Gabe heaved another shovelful of ashes into the containment bin near the Health Spa.

The construction crew thought he was crazy for volunteering to cleanup the ashes from the fire but he needed to do this.

He'd been doing cleanup since they got back from their visit with Rory's half brother.

Something had been nagging him every since they had talked with Ned. Something about Rory's Aunt Mal. He needed to call Max Harrison today and have him look into it.

Meanwhile he would finish cleaning up these ashes.

This was something he could do that was easy to fix.

The broken relationship between him and his wife was not.

His fake wife.

Rory had reminded him of that. She wanted things to go back to their original agreement.

A marriage-of-convenience.

Strictly business.

A sudden burst of awareness unfolded deep inside of him. The original agreement wasn't what he wanted anymore.

Gabe was beginning to realize he wanted a whole lot more.

He wanted the old Rory back. The woman who laughed at his jokes, played with dogs on the beach and sat close to him or walked beside him listening to his passions and plans for the future.

This distant and emotionless Rory — the woman she had become since their talk — was a stranger to him.

Since returning from their trip to Oregon five days ago they had hardly talked at all. Their meals together were stilted and silent.

Mrs. O'Toole still made her delicious meals but Gabe couldn't enjoy them with his thoughts so wrapped up in how to fix things with his wife.

As he finished shovelling the last of the ashes into the bin he stood still for a moment staring at the huge pile of cinders.

Right now his relationship with Rory looked like that. It was black and grey with no color.

Could beauty still come from something that looked dead and lifeless?

He hoped so.

In fact he was counting on it.

Hurrying home Gabe decided needed to talk to Jack. His brother might look like a pirate with his scarred cheek but he had an uncanny sense about people.

Grand said Jack was born with good horse sense. He had a gut feeling about people and an insight into what made them tick.

He was counting on Jack's good horse sense today.

Entering through the side door by the kitchen he heard their cook humming softly like she usually did. Somehow it made their house a little more cheery.

Following the scent of freshly baked cookies Gabe walked into the kitchen and grabbed a warm one off the counter.

"These smell delicious Mrs. O'Toole." Gabe smiled as he took a bite. "And taste even better."

Their cook swatted him with a spatula. "Oh go on with you then, Gabe Stevenson." He liked that she swatted him and had a little fun. He never got tired of hearing her Irish brogue.

Gabe winked at her smiling face as he swallowed rest of his cookie. Turning he went down the long hallway toward his office.

Passing Rory's office he stopped for a moment. The click-clack of her fingers typing away on the computer was all he heard. He decided he wouldn't disturb her as she was probably in the middle of a train of thought and wouldn't appreciate the interruption.

Walking into his office at the end of the hall he closed the door. Pulling out his phone he called Jack.

"Jack here."

"Hey pirate." Jack's good-natured chuckle at the end of the line reminded him of their strong bond as brothers.

"Gabe. It's good to hear from you." Jack's voice was unhurried and helped to settle Gabe's nerves.

"It's been awhile. Do you have time to talk?"

"My time is yours, bro."

Gabe explained the heated conversation between Rory and him on the way back from seeing her half brother. "I just don't understand why she would feel like I should've married a model or a woman with more sophistication or a better pedigree. I like Rory because she's real and doesn't put on airs."

"Did you tell her that?"

"Yes but it didn't seem to change anything. She still feels like I married her because I felt sorry for her."

Jack was silent for a moment. "Sounds to me like your wife is running scared. Seems like she's backing away from you because she doesn't feel like she fits into your world of influence and wealth. She's like a skittish colt who has ran through a fire before and been burned and is terrified of it happening again. Maybe everything that's going on with her half brother Ned combined with the newness of being married to you has cut her heart open until she's raw and vulnerable. Maybe she is afraid of the closeness between you and her."

"That's sounds about right." Gabe paced his office floor realizing that was probably true. "So how do I fix this

Jack? How do I get my wife to learn to trust me and get back to growing that close bond between us?"

"Be kind and patient with Rory. From the sounds of things she's just been hurt one too many times." Jack continued, "And most important of all? Show her in every way you can how much you love her."

Gabe stopped pacing staring out the window. He stood silent for a full minute mulling over Jack's words.

Jack chuckled on the other end. "Don't be shocked. It's as plain as day that you love her. Show her that. And when the time is right tell her."

Expelling a slow breath Gabe closed his eyes as he realized the truth of Jack's words. "You make it sound easy. It's really tough to lay your heart on the line. There's always the possibility that it'll get crushed." He rubbed the back of his neck as he stared out the window at the water below.

"True enough. But that's why you need to dig deeper and ask yourself if you can live without her. When you know the answer to that you can run after what you really want."

"Jack you have an uncanny sense about people. Thanks for your advice." It was at times like this Gabe appreciated his brother more than words could say.

"Anytime man. Oh and we'll see you at the pier around noon?"

"Yes we'll be there."

"See you later then."

Gabe hung up grateful for Jack's advice. Now all he had to do was take it. It might be one of the most difficult things he'd done yet.

He wanted to tell Rory how he felt about her right now but that would need to wait.

They had to hurry to the Yacht. Tonight was her surprise birthday party and they needed to be away from the Lodge for a few hours so the people he hired could set things up.

Her actual birthday wasn't until tomorrow but he needed to have the party a day ahead because he had to fly out tomorrow. He'd agreed to go on a six-week speaking tour for Cyrus Noble's chain of Hotels and Resorts.

Problem was he still hadn't told Rory.

He hoped there would be time to talk to her tonight. Mentally Gabe began to rehearse all the things he wanted to tell his wife.

Gabe wanted to tell her that since he'd met her how his life had changed. It was true. Rory had a way of bringing him down to earth. She made him feel like he was grounded and rooted in something strong, something meaningful and something worth fighting for.

Something like the love he had for her.

He hadn't told her yet but he would. He would show her how much he loved her, expressing all the deep emotions of his heart.

Somehow he needed to let his wife know how much she meant to him even if she was convinced they were done sharing their messy emotions.

RORY STOOD beside Gabe on the bridge of his Yacht.

He had convinced her that they should take advantage of the sunny day.

At first she didn't really want to go because that would mean she would need to be in close quarters with Gabe. Since they returned five days ago from talking with her half brother, she had barely spoken with her husband.

She didn't know how much longer she could go on with this chilly atmosphere between them. And the sad part was she didn't have anyone to blame but herself.

Still, she was aware of the desperate need to guard her heart. She didn't want to be hurt. Getting close to Gabe only to be rejected or abandoned again would lead down the path straight to heartache.

Rory sighed heavily.

This afternoon Gabe seemed to be in a good mood and was being very attentive and kind to her.

How much longer would she be able to keep her heart aloof?

"Do you want to take the helm?" Gabe grinned at her and stood back from the wheel.

She hesitated for a moment. "Are you sure? I've only ever steered the sailboat."

"Being behind the helm of the yacht is similar at least for what we're doing today." Gabe assured her and stepped back.

She stepped behind the wheel and took over. Gabe's state-of-the-art modern yacht was incredible. The bridge sat higher up and when she was at the helm she could see for miles across the water.

"This feels amazing." She breathed out a happy sigh and looked at him.

Gabe eyes were riveted on her a new warmth in his eyes. "It is."

Feeling disconcerted, Rory turned back to look straight ahead. "Where are we headed?"

"To Paradise Lake." Her husband's blue eyes sparkled.

"Is it a surprise?"

"You might say that." Gabe chuckled. "You'll find out soon enough. I can see our destination just up ahead."

Tingles went up her spine starting from where Gabe placed a warm hand on the small of her back.

Before long they were docking at the long pier for yachts.

Hearing loud voices she looked up.

"We'd better get outside to greet them."

"Surprise Rory! Happy Birthday from all of us." Bella was waving at her and Gabe as they stepped from the yacht onto the pier.

"Ah thank you everyone. This is a wonderful surprise." Her eyes brimmed with unshed tears. She'd never had this many people telling her happy birthday in her life.

Gabe's whole family was there as well as her friend Raz.

"But don't get too comfortable because we're all coming back with you to Walker's Island." Raz giggled wrapping her in her arms.

"You are?"

"She's right. We're headed back. Your aunts will be waiting at the Lodge when we get there." Gabe grinned.

"Oh this is so much fun." Rory grinned happy to see Raz and Gabe's family.

They stepped onto the yacht and it was a little over an

hour before they walked onto the Island toward Grand's Hunting Lodge.

Rory could hear country music as they neared their home.

Rounding the corner she peered into the large back yard to see one of her favorite country bands warming up. She saw all sorts of fun birthday games setup in the backyard.

She was reminded of the fact that she'd told Gabe of her dream to have a big birthday party where there were all sorts of fun things to do.

"Did you plan all of this?" Rory turned to Gabe, her eyes big and round.

Gabe chuckled. "Of course. With a little help from your friend Razelle and your aunts."

"Thank you. This looks like so much fun." Rory gave Gabe a kiss on the cheek and then hugged Raz.

All three of her aunts stood in front of a large table with snacks and drinks.

"Thank you." She hugged them each in turn.

Aunt Merrie soon called everyone to attention. Telling them it was time to start. They had set up a small mini-golf course but there were a few backyard games like a large wooden Jenga, donut-eating on a string, a photo booth area that hung from a tree and a huge piñata.

Luke and Zach, Gabe's younger brothers were soon having a great time donut eating on a string while Bella and Elle started playing the large-sized Jenga game. Gabe had joined Adam and Jack to play a round of mini-golf.

Rory and Raz joined Bella and Elle for a game of Jenga. Trying to pull out a piece of two by four wood without letting the tower fall was difficult. First time through Rory was the player who made the tower fall but she got better the more times they played.

Before long Aunt Merrie announced that it was time for the scavenger hunt. She gave each person a paper with a picture on it. Everyone had ten minutes to find the item and get back in time. First person back won the game.

Rory's picture was of a pinecone, a flower and something blue. She hurried toward the back of the house and into the area where there were a lot of trees certain she would find pinecones there.

The sun was still shining as she walked into the bushes.

Walking deeper into the forested area she stopped in front of a pine tree. She grabbed onto a couple branches and shook them until a few pinecones fell onto the ground.

Bending over she picked up a couple of pinecones only to see something shiny laying on the ground beside it.

A shiny gold bracelet with a heart shaped locket glinted from the rays of sun that poked through the trees.

She picked up the both items. The gold bracelet seemed quite old and she wondered where it came from. Turning it over she read the inscription on the back. *To our daughter Mallory Murphy, love Mama and Papa.*

Suddenly the hairs on the back of her neck bristled as she stood there.

It felt like she was being watched.

Hurrying out of the forested area she followed the sounds of laughter until she came to the backyard.

Raz was already celebrating her win when Rory got

back. She stopped and read the inscription again, remembering what she'd read in her mother's diary this morning.

I don't know if I should invite my sister Mal to Rory's sixth birthday party. The last few birthday parties she's attended, she was so mean to me and to our little Rory.

She always calls Rory Delanie's precious princess who gets everything. Mal is constantly complaining about how much I fuss over Rory and that Mal never had anyone to fuss over her.

Sometimes I wonder if all those years when my sister Mal had to deal with our father's drunken rages caused something to snap inside her.

Maybe resentment and bitterness from all those abusive years have built up to the point that now she's decided she wants her revenge.

I'm worried about Edward and Rory and our safety. I don't think I'll invite her to our daughter's birthday party.

Rory shivered as she thought of the implications. If this bracelet belonged to Aunt Mal it meant that at some point she had been here on the Island. She'd been near their house.

Her fingers traced the contours of the heart-shaped locket that hung around her neck staring at the bracelet that matched it.

Why is Aunt Mal here? And if she was here why didn't she visit her sisters?

"Hey birthday girl are you okay?" As Gabe walked up to her Rory quickly put the bracelet into her pocket.

She didn't know why she hid the bracelet. Maybe it was because she didn't want Gabe to worry about her and feel like he needed to protect her even more.

She forced a smile desperate for Gabe to believe that everything was normal. "Yes. This is a fun day."

A furrow formed on his forehead. "Hmm. You seem a little worried about something."

"I'm good. Oh look, Mrs. O'Toole is bringing out the birthday cake." Everyone started singing happy birthday and Rory was grateful for the distraction.

She blew out the candles, but there was still one candle left burning.

"How sweet Gabe, Rory left one candle burning for you." Eliza Stevenson smiled happily.

"Yes she has and I couldn't be happier."

Heat rushed to Rory's cheeks as she peered up into her husband's eyes. Blue eyes that burned with intense heat and longing gazed back at her.

Shaken to her core, Rory quickly blew the last remaining candle out.

After all the fun and games were over the country band started playing.

Gabe reached for her hand kissing the back of it. "May I have this dance, my lady?"

"Of course good sir." Rory did a little curtsy and Gabe put one arm around her waist pulling her close. She was enjoying it all too much being in her husband's arms.

He pulled her closer and whispered in her ear. "I hope this has been a special birthday for you."

"It has been special thank you. The last big birthday I had was my sixth birthday which had a horrible ending." Her voice shook with the memory of her parent's dying in the house fire.

"I'm sorry Rory. You must miss them so much."

Rory swallowed back tears. "Yes. Even though it's been years, I still miss them."

"I hope the time spent today with your aunts, Raz and my family has helped take away some of your loneliness."

"It has." Rory leaned against her husband enjoying his closeness while she could. She knew all too soon that their relationship would return to the detached lives they had been living.

Watching her aunts dance with the Stevenson brothers made her happy. She was glad they were having fun. Even Raz was enjoying a slow country dance with Gabe's brother Luke.

If the smile on her friend's face was any indication Raz was definitely enjoying herself.

It was late in the evening before everyone started leaving the party. The band packed up and left on their boat. Gabe had given Adam the keys to the yacht and he took everyone else back to Paradise Lake.

Gabe and Rory walked her three aunts back to their cottage. When they got back to the Lodge and opened the door, all was quiet.

Rory missed the excitement and fun of friends and family.

"Well I'm tired, but it's a good tired. Thank you so much Gabe. What a wonderful surprise." Rory took off her shoes and rested for a moment on the living room chair.

"I'm glad. Before you go to bed, I need to tell you something."

Rory braced herself at the serious look on his face. "What's up?"

"I've agreed to go do a six week trip with Cyrus Noble speaking for the Noble Hotel and Resort conferences." Gabe's brows puckered in worry.

"I had no idea." Anxiety that had been buried in her belly sprung out of hiding. "Six weeks?"

"Yes. I know it's a long time. And I'm sorry for springing this on you. If you want to you could go visit Raz or invite her here. Or you could go stay with your aunts if you like."

"No, I'll stay here. I have lots to take care of. When do you leave?" She fidgeted nervously with her hands.

"I leave in an hour. My pilot just landed the plane on the airstrip and is waiting for me."

Rory stood to her feet her legs trembling. She breathed out slowly, trying to calm the fear that was building inside her.

She steadied herself by putting a hand against the wall behind her. Her husband was about to abandon her for six weeks.

Who knew when or if he'd be back?

"I hope you have a safe trip Gabe." Her voice wobbled and she swallowed hurriedly hoping her husband wouldn't notice her raw emotions.

"You don't need to worry about me, I'll be fine." To Rory's dismay her voice cracked but she forced a smile.

He stood to his feet. Deep lines formed on his forehead, his blue eyes intense as he stared at her for a long moment. "You're sure you'll be okay?"

"I'll be fine." She didn't trust herself to speak anymore or she would dissolve into a puddle of tears.

Her husband nodded. Leaning down he kissed her cheek. "I'll be back as soon as I can, I promise."

Rory stared at his back as he hurried away.

Her eyes flooded with tears.

Of everyone that had left today she hoped Gabe would stay most of all.

He'd become her safe place and her friend.

The birthday party had been lovely but in the end she would end up alone on her birthday after all.

Once again — just like when she was six years old — she was abandoned on her birthday.

Tears fell and she hurried to her bedroom.

Without even changing her clothes she crawled under the covers, her shoulders shaking with heart wrenching sobs of being left alone again.

What was the matter with her?

Was she destined to be married to a man who would abandon her?

Maybe Maddie Winslow got it right after all. Her horrible words came back to haunt her. *Gabe married a poor little Island girl with no class or culture. You won't stay married to him for long. He needs a woman who will help him get to the top, not drag him down. Someone with more to offer than you.*

Maybe she really wasn't good enough for Gabe.

Maybe she really wasn't a woman who had anything good to offer him.

Maybe she really wasn't worthy to be loved.

GABE SETTLED his head back against the cushioned seat on his private jet and tried to get comfortable.

He was too keyed up to rest.

His thoughts went through all the speaking commitments he had for this series of conferences.

Speaking at these conferences for Noble Hotels and Resorts would help expand his audience and would help give him access into the Hotel and Resort Industry.

This really was a once-in-a-lifetime opportunity.

A dream fulfilled.

Then why didn't he feel excited?

A memory returned of his last look at Rory's pale face as she stood in front of him.

Gabe thought he saw her lips tremble even as she smiled at him. And her beautiful violet eyes instead of being soft and warm were unnaturally bright almost as if she was scared of something.

What would cause his wife to be afraid?

His thoughts swirled with memories of Rory's birthday party tonight. They had fun and even danced a slow dance together, but he didn't really get closer to his wife tonight. It seemed like she was still distancing herself from him.

When she stepped out of the trees on her way back to the party, her face had looked pale and her hands were shaking.

What had happened from the time she was at the birthday party to when she stepped into the forested area behind the Lodge?

Rory had already gone to bed by the time he had packed his suitcase and got ready to leave the house.

As he bent down to get his shoes on, he'd seen an old gold bracelet lying on the floor. Picking it up he read the engraved words on the back of it. *To our daughter Mallory Murphy, love Mama and Papa.*

Who was Mallory Murphy?

Questions had tumbled around in his mind ever since he'd got on the airplane. He tried to remember every conversation he'd had with Rory or her three aunts.

When he'd first met them they had been concerned about their niece's safety. They had said something about her father having a mistress, which had proven true. The result had been Rory's half brother Ned.

Slowly a memory of his conversation with Aunt Merrie came back to him. *Rory's Aunt Mal complained that Delanie's little princess got everything that should have come to her, but never did.* There was definitely some bitterness and resentment between the sisters.

But something else nagged at him.

It was when they were at the police station when Rory was talking to Ned. He had mentioned her Aunt Mal. What had his wife's half brother said? *Your Aunt Mal contacted me and suggested I scare you a little that it might help me feel better knowing that my half sister was getting a little of what she deserved.*

The bracelet belonged to Rory's Aunt Mal. If his wife found the bracelet in the forested area behind the Hunting Lodge it could only mean one thing.

Gabe lurched upright in his seat and called out.

"David I need you to turn the plane back around. We need to get back to Walker's Island. And hurry." Gabe's voice called out to his pilot his voice sounding strained to his own ears.

"Sure thing Mr. Stevenson. Estimated time of arrival is thirty minutes." His pilot responded quickly.

Gabe's fingers gripped the armrest his knuckles turning white as the planed turned around in suddenly.

He sent up a prayer that Rory would be safe. That he wouldn't arrive too late to save his wife.

CHAPTER FIFTEEN

ory

"MOMMY WHERE ARE YOU? *I can't see you. It's hard to breathe. Please come help me." She woke up with a scream and sat straight up in bed panic hitting her. Smoke filled the room and she could hardly breathe. Scurrying off her bed she ran from her room out into the hallway.*

"Daddy?" Her hands shook as she ran them along the wall that led to her parents' bedroom. Fits of coughing soon followed. Where was Mommy? Why wasn't Daddy answering her? How come she could hardly breathe?

She called again only no one answered.

Sweat formed on her forehead as heat and flashes of fire spewed from the big crack in the door. She was about to touch the door when someone grabbed her by the shoulders...

The familiar dream came back and she woke up screaming.

Suddenly she started coughing until her shoulders shook. Waking up her eyes watered. She could hardly breathe.

Smoke flooded her bedroom.

A faint barking sounded from outside her window. Why were her dogs outside? Rory was sure they had been in her room when she fell asleep last night.

Without warning, a woman's loud cackle-like laughter echoed off the walls.

"Your mommy and daddy aren't going to save you this time princess. In fact no one is." A deep grainy voice uttered a threat that sounded like a death-knell in Rory's ears.

Fear coiled in her belly at the woman's words. She rubbed her eyes straining to see who was speaking. But it was no use.

She couldn't see anything in the dark smoke-filled room.

"Who are you? What do you want?" She could hear the quiver in her own voice.

"My darling girl. Don't you remember me? I'm your dear Aunt Mal." Her laugh was reckless and bawdy. "Of course your mother never approved of me. I know that because she hardly ever invited me to any of your birthday parties."

Rory lay there silent for a moment. Then she remembered. The bracelet she'd found last night.

An intuitive feeling told her that her Aunt Mal had

been on the Island. But Rory never expected her aunt to try to harm her.

"Aunt Mal. I remember you used to stop by and read me stories. I was about four I think." Rory spoke of fond memories without thinking.

"Yes silly me. That was fun for a time. Then my sister — your mom — said I complained too much when I came to visit so she stopped inviting me. But it especially made me angry when your Mom stopped inviting me to your birthday parties. Suddenly I was no longer part of the family. You, their only princess was more important. No longer was I valued. No longer was I loved."

"That's not true…"

Aunt Mal screeched at her. "It was true!" Suddenly her voice went eerily soft. "But I took care of that on your sixth birthday when I showed up anyway."

"How come I don't remember seeing you that night?" Her sixth birthday party was quite vivid in her mind. For some reason her Aunt Mal's red hair and green eyes didn't come back to her memory.

"Because I snuck in by the back door. I was hiding in your Dad's office. You see I was very clever." Her Aunt's voice lilted upwards in a childish way as she giggled at her own cleverness.

"I watched from the crack in the door. I saw you blow out your candles and I even saw when your mom put your grandmother's gold heart-shaped locket necklace around your neck."

Aunt Mal's voice suddenly switched to anger. "That was supposed to be my necklace from my mother. It matched my bracelet. I earned it when I took all of the beatings from my drunken father. It should've been mine. But no, your Grand-mother decided to give it to Delanie instead of me. Then for your sixth birthday your Mom decided to give it to you."

Her hands fisted the locket around her neck, her hands shaking. Rory looked fondly back on that time when her mom placed the locket around her neck and held it as a treasured memory.

Her mom had added pictures of Rory's Dad and Mom inside this heart-shaped pendant.

All these years later she still loved the feel of the locket hanging around her neck. It was a way of keeping the love of her parents close by her side throughout childhood.

Smoke increased in the room and Rory released a hacking cough.

Her Aunt Mal continued talking as if nothing changed. "But when I saw you were given the necklace I decided it was my time to take control. So I did."

She laughed insanely. "As soon as everyone went to bed your parents stood on the balcony of their bedroom. I snuck in and lit candles and set the curtains on fire that covered the balcony door. They were trapped."

Rory let out an anguished cry. "Why? Why did you do that? I loved my parents."

"Because they didn't treat me like family. They didn't give me those things I deserved. They didn't value me. So they deserved to be treated the same way they treated me… with disdain and cruelty."

Aunt Mal's evil cackle echoed through the room. It was a long time before she quieted. Footsteps approached the bed. "So this time it's you who is doomed to die. But not before I get what I came for."

Without warning Rory felt long cold fingers reach for her fumbling until they came to her neck. With a sudden jerk she felt the necklace around her neck snap in two.

"I have it now. It's mine now forever. Besides you won't need it where you're going." The woman's cold calculated laugh sent terror through Rory's veins.

Hysterical laughter echoed through her bedroom and down the hallway as Aunt Mal walked away.

Scrambling off the bed, Rory tried to find her way to the door through the thick haze of smoke.

Her whole body was shivering, trembling and quaking.

Heat from the fire pelted her skin like thousands of tiny rocks hitting her all at once. Darkness surrounded her except for the orange-red glow of light from the fire.

All she could think of as smoke and heat increased in the room was that she'd lost everything she ever wanted.

Tears fell down her cheeks mixing unheeded with the smoke and fire that surrounded her.

First she'd lost her parents who both died leaving her alone. Then she found out she had a half brother who did his best to scare her and an Aunt who hated her enough to kill her. But the last loss was the most devastating.

Losing Gabe.

He might have rescued her with a marriage promise but she had grown to love him. Now she realized her love had blinded her to the truth.

She was someone who wasn't worthy to be Gabe's wife.

Instead, she was someone for Gabe to feel sorry for in the same way his friend Billy had been all those years ago.

Her husband might even believe that he had started to feel something more for her right now, but time would prove him wrong.

Gabe's mother said that it didn't take him long to shift his interest to other friends. She was convinced the same thing would happen to her.

There was no guarantee that things would be different with her, that within a few short weeks or months her husband wouldn't regret that he'd married her.

But, none of that mattered anymore.

It was too late for her dream. It was too late for her marriage. It was too late for her to love.

She barely made it a few steps before she collapsed and lay still.

Memories of reaching out for her parents in that smoke-filled hallway when she was little girl came back to her before the darkness closed in.

Pouring rain peppered Gabe's skin as he hurried down the steps of his private jet.

He could hardly see his way clear as he ran down the trail that led to the Lodge.

He'd already called the emergency dispatch number. The police, ambulance and fire fighters were on their way.

As he got closer to their home he saw an orange-red glow from the windows and flames licking their corners.

Please God let me save my wife in time. I love her. I want her to live. I want to have her by my side.

Rushing through the kitchen door he hurried up the stairs. The fire was raging from his bedroom and out into the hallway.

It was impossible to get through that way.

He rushed outside and grabbing a ladder from the shed he set it against the wall near the window to Rory's bedroom.

Using a hammer he smashed the glass on the window careful to make sure all the glass along the window pane was crushed.

He scurried up and inside Rory's bedroom. A thick haze of smoke filled the room and he could hardly breathe.

Climbing down from the window he couldn't see anything in the smoke filled room. Gabe stretched out his hands in the dark to find Rory. He searched the bed but she wasn't there.

Next, he got on the floor and crawled on his hands and knees determined to find his wife.

Suddenly he reached out touching something soft.

His wife lay there.

"Rory can you hear me?" He leaned down to talk to her but all was silent.

She lay motionless.

He needed to get her out of here. Fast.

Lifting his wife up he carried her to the window.

Climbing through the window he held her so she wouldn't fall then carried her over his shoulder as he went down the ladder.

As soon as his feet touched the ground he hurried over to the guest cottage where their cook lived. He needed to get Rory out of the rain to help her.

Mrs. O'Toole answered the door as soon as he knocked. Seeing that he carried Rory she hurried to open the door. "Lay her on my bed. The poor lassie. We need to get her better."

Rory lay on the bed white as a sheet. Gabe heard the sounds of the helicopter landing on the Island.

"Mrs. O'Toole, I just heard the emergency helicopter. Would you go tell the emergency crew Rory needs immediate care?" Gabe turned to her and she nodded quickly slipping on her shoes and hurrying out the door.

Turning quickly to Rory he remembered what he'd learned from his first aid training years ago. He slid two fingers to the side of her neck and could feel a faint but steady pulse. Leaning down he listened for her breathing but only heard shallow breaths.

She still wasn't moving so he tilted her head back, closed her nose with two fingers and opened her mouth. Setting his lips to hers he breathed oxygen into her lungs.

He puffed two quick breaths into her mouth and checked her. It was only after he repeated the process two more times that Rory inhaled a deep breath.

"Rory." Gabe ground out her name as though in torment and reached for his wife hauling her into his arms with the force of his need.

All the pent up fears and worries came suddenly crashing down on Gabe. "I thought I'd lost you. I nearly went mad with fear."

"Aunt Mal... set fire." Rory breathed out tears running down her cheeks.

"I know. I'm so sorry." Gabe kissed the top of her head, his arms trembling from the weight of the crushing fear they both had been through.

"You're back. You can't. You'll miss that speaking commitment." She coughed for a long time trying to clear her airway.

Gabe helped her sip some water. "I care more about you than some speaking engagement. I'm so thankful you're alive." He leaned his forehead on hers and sighed heavily.

"Does that mean you forgive me for pulling away and being so distant?" Rory's large violet eyes were tear-filled and solemn.

"Of course I forgive you." Gabe swallowed back the emotion that threatened to consume him. He pulled her onto his lap raining kisses on her eyelids and cheeks. "I finally realized today when I nearly lost you how much you mean to me."

His chest heaved and his eyes closed trying to shut out the vivid images of the fire burning up his home, convinced Rory had died.

Gabe's hands stroked her hair as he released jagged breaths. He kissed her forehead once more.

"Heaven help me Rory, but once I realized your Aunt Mal meant to harm you I couldn't get to you fast enough."

He looked deeply into his wife's eyes and expelling a shaky breath, shut his eyes for a brief moment.

Rory cried softly into her husband's shoulder her arms encircling his neck.

His hand moved in gentle circles along her back.

"I'm so happy you came back for me. You didn't abandon me." Rory whispered a sudden sob escaping as she had imagined he might be gone for good.

"I won't ever abandon you my beautiful wife." Gabe kissed the top of her head cradling her close.

"Gabe," Rory whispered her mouth so close to his that their breath mingled. "Thank you for rescuing me."

She pulled away so she could see Gabe. Rory reached a hand up and touched his cheek staring into her husband's haunted eyes.

Gabe nodded, his eyes pained refusing to leave her face. Then ever so slowly, almost as if he expected her to pull away, her husband moved his lips closer to hers. "I can't stand the thought of losing you. I'd rather die myself."

Rory turned her face to accept his kiss unable to deny him anything.

Shaky hands tangled suddenly in her thick blonde hair holding her captive, his lips ravaging hers with an intensity that sent her senses reeling.

Nothing mattered in this moment except the warmth of her husband's touch. A fierce tenderness rose up on the inside as Rory fervently fed his need.

Gabe's heartfelt whisper caused her to come undone. "My sweet Rory I love you. I can't bear to lose you."

"You won't. I'm here... I'm here." Her body molded to her husband's and she offered her lips to his loving mastery. Over and over he kissed her until she was breathless.

Rory's arms reached up encircling his neck drawing him closer.

It was this deep devotion that she had longed for from the start. Her heart basked in the realization that Gabe needed her.

Gabe pulled his mouth from hers with a low moan as if unwilling to part from her for one moment. His strong arms cradled her close to his chest and she could hear the rapid beating of his heart. A deep sense of happiness and contentment filled her.

Her husband continued to stroke her hair and Rory snuggled closer to his heart.

Rory loved being held by her husband but there was something even more powerful about the tender way he held her now.

She sensed a deeper connection to Gabe almost like their souls bonded in a way they hadn't before.

Her husband had told her he'd become attached to her, but it was only now that she'd finally believed him. Rory swallowed back the emotion that threatened to consume her.

They sat together in the stillness for a long time. She cherished this time of closeness with her husband.

"I'm sorry too for the times when I pulled away from you. I was scared of being vulnerable to love. My heart was on the line and I was afraid." Gabe's gruff whisper broke through the stillness of the moment.

"I told you how I lost my father and my friend Billy, but I've finally realized that all that pain and heartache made me too afraid to love. A big part of that pain has been my fear of losing someone I love again."

She felt the weight of Gabe's sorrow in his words.

"It's okay Gabe." Rory tightened her grip around his waist aware of how difficult it must be for him to speak of the death of his friend and father.

Her husband's body tensed. "No it's not okay, Rory. Don't you see? I don't want to hide from love. But I failed to truly love and protect my Dad and Billy the way they needed me to. What if I fail you too? My heart couldn't take it if I lost you too."

Rory put her hands on his cheeks and looked her husband in the eyes. "Listen to me. It wasn't your fault Billy decided to take the dare from the popular kids and dive that day. It wasn't your fault that your Dad passed away from the heart attack." Rory moved back a little ways to look into Gabe's eyes her own cloudy with unshed tears.

"But it was. I've always felt responsible for them both." Gabe pressed his eyes shut a harsh groan falling from his lips. "For years the weight of their deaths has all but crushed me. I'm terrified that somehow I'll repeat the same mistakes with you because I love you so much that it scares me to live day after day in a world without you in it."

He expelled a labored breath. "Which is why I've decided to do everything I can to change. But, I might need your help. I want to be vulnerable and close to you. I want to spend a lifetime learning how to love you Rory."

A single tear slipped down her cheek. Her husband

reached over and with gentle fingers wiped away her tears.

She turned to look into her husband's eyes.

"You love me?"

"I think I fell in love with you when we went sailing together a couple weeks ago. It was so wonderful having you by my side that I longed to sail away and never look back. And it's also why I've been so bad-tempered all this time as I've tried my best to push you away and ignore these feelings." Gabe ran a shaky hand through his hair and grimaced. "I'm sorry for that."

Rory was thrilled to hear her husband's words of love. "I forgive you. I love you with all my heart."

Gabe pulled her closer and kissed her briefly. "I've been drawn to you from the first. You're a woman who is warm, gentle and kind. Someone who also happens to be selfless, beautiful and very... captivating." Her husband faltered on the last word as his eyes darkened and moved down to her lips.

Rory swallowed back emotion at his words forcing herself to meet his gaze.

He whispered words mingled close to her lips. He kissed both of her eyelids, her cheeks and her nose before he spoke. "I want to ask you something."

"What?" She asked, breathless.

"When we first married we agreed that this would be a fake marriage. Now the tide has shifted and we've fallen in love." Gabe leaned his forehead against hers, his eyes squeezing shut a hesitation in his voice. "Do you think you would mind being married for real to rogue like me?"

Rory let out the breath she'd been holding while the corners of her mouth turned up an invitation on her lips.

Her husband's fierce love for her coupled with his need to have her as his forever wife was the most compelling reason to make this marriage real. "Gabe you're not a rogue... you're the man I love. You've rescued me, you've trusted me with the most vulnerable part of yourself and you've honored me by loving me. More than anything I would be happy to be your wife in every way."

The tender passion she saw in his eyes caused a shiver to run up her spine.

Her husband's lips touched her own with a sweet reckless abandon. Gabe's arms tightened around her and embraced her close. His hands reached up to cradle her face large blue eyes darkening and searching hers a hesitation in his movements.

Rory reached up and brushed her lips against his, her kisses saying much more than words ever could.

Gabe groaned unable to wait a second longer he folded her in his arms, kissing her with the hunger of a starved man. "Rory my beautiful wife. You're mine forever. I love you."

"I love you too my wonderful husband." Rory's heart raced at her husband's passionate kisses.

So many emotions rose up inside her. And her heart overflowed with love.

CHAPTER SIXTEEN

*ne year later...*

"THANK you family and friends for coming to the Grand Opening of *The Princess Rory Hotel and Resort.*" Gabe Stevenson stood beside his wife in front of a large crowd that had gathered to celebrate this new beginning.

He chuckled and glanced at the massive five-story building behind him. "As you can see it was important for us to make sure we could make room for a whole lot of guests. So you are all welcome to be our guests tonight free of charge."

The crowd applauded and shouted their appreciation.

"I named this Hotel and Resort in honor of my beautiful wife Rory. Her compassion and strength have always been an inspiration to me." Gabe paused as his gaze swept over his wife and their new baby daughter in appreciation.

Rory's violet eyes sparkled with happiness and in her arms she held their new blue-eyed daughter.

He swallowed as emotion caught his throat. "Many of you might remember we had a harrowing beginning to the construction of this Resort and my wife almost didn't make it. However thanks to the emergency crew she is healthy and has added a new addition to our family — our daughter Delanie Eliza Stevenson."

He looked over the crowd pleased to see all of his family, Rory's three aunts and her half brother Ned. Cyrus and Anna Noble were there as well as Grand's old lawyer and his wife.

Rory's friends had joined them as well as several of the Paradise Lake emergency workers and some of the town council. Dan Summers and his new wife Amy had joined them too. Maria and her brother Juan had moved to Walker's Island from Argentina to join their staff of workers.

Today it felt like they were celebrating with friends.

"For today's events we thought we would have a tour of the hotel and grounds. By the time we meet back here the caterers will have the food ready. Sound good?"

Gabe grinned at the loud applause. "Follow me."

He put his arm around Rory and they walked into the Hotel. Standing in the massive foyer he heard loud gasps from the crowd as their gaze lifted to see many large windows that reached five stories high.

"You can tell we like it sunny and bright here." The crowd laughed. "As you can see to my left is the reception area and past that on this main floor is the staff rooms, a kitchen, the laundry and maintenance rooms. To my right is a wide hallway that leads to a large tea room and restaurant."

The guests followed Gabe and Rory into the restaurant with its spacious tables, high ceilings and brightly colored floor patterns.

Next to the restaurant was a spacious coffee shop that included a large stage area for musical guests and other artists as well as large bookshop.

"This is so beautiful." Raz walked close to Rory, her arms waving as she pointed out little delights in the room. "There is so much color here. I'll need to pass along some of these ideas to my Mother. Maybe we could make our little coffee shop more appealing."

Razelle turned to look at her mother who was alert as usual and keeping a constant watch over her daughter.

They came at last to a large room on the other side where there was an indoor Olympic sized pool that included a kids pool and two hot tubs.

"This is stunning. I need to plan my next vacation here." One of the guests from Paradise Lake blurted out.

Thrilled with the happy response Gabe led the group back outside to the Health Spa. It was a separate building and a beautifully large space.

So many people were happily talking about planning their next vacation at their Hotel and Resort and it thrilled him.

Outside once again Gabe pointed to the caterers who stood behind tables laden heavy with food. "That's it for the tour. I hope you enjoyed it. Please help yourself to food and drinks."

People lined up for the food quickly and Gabe put his arm around Rory. "How was that?"

"Wonderful as usual my love." Rory kissed him quickly and held out their little girl. He pulled the tiny bundle into his arms.

"Ah sweet goodness." Gabe leaned close to his daughter and kissed her forehead. "Fast asleep. I guess my speech must have been pretty boring after all."

Rory giggled. "No silly. Babies sleep a lot. Our little Delanie has been such a good baby."

Eliza Stevenson walked up to them and gently plucked the tiny blanket away from her granddaughter's face. "Ah she is so beautiful. Gabe let me hold my namesake for a little while. You two have a break and enjoy yourselves."

"Thanks Mom." Gabe placed the baby in her arms and grabbed Rory's hand. "We'll do that."

Gabe was happy just holding her hand.

"What do you say we escape the crowd for a little while and take a walk on the beach?" Gabe whispered in his wife's ear.

Rory looked around a little unsure. "We can do that? All these people are expecting us to be here."

"Sweetheart, it's okay if we go for walk. But if it makes you feel better I'll let someone know where we've gone." Gabe hurried over to let Adam and Jack know they were taking a walk. He also let his Mom know she could text him if little Delanie needed them back.

"We're good to go. Let's get out of here." Gabe winked at Rory and they walked toward the beach.

It was a beautiful sunny day and he needed to enjoy some time with his charming wife.

He was still so thankful that Rory was alive and healthy after her close call one year ago.

The Emergency response team had found Rory's Aunt Mal lying face down in the forested area behind the Lodge. She was cold as ice and barely breathing with the locket still fisted tightly in her hand.

After she'd been at the Hospital for a week, the Doctor had pronounced her well enough, but had insisted on a Psychiatric evaluation. She was diagnosed with bipolar disorder and schizophrenia as well as numerous other mental disorders.

"What did the Doctor say about your Aunt Mal when you saw her last week?" Gabe squeezed his wife's hand gently realizing it was still hard for her to talk about it.

"She's still the same. Day after day she talks about all the things that should have been hers and who hurt her. The Doctor said it's like she's reverted to living like an angry child. The medication has helped calm her though." Rory grimaced and sighed heavily as she fingered the gold locket at her neck.

The police had given it back to her broken, but her husband had fixed the heart-locket necklace for her.

She was so grateful.

"I'm sorry. It's been hard on you."

Rory nodded. "Thank you for understanding Gabe. But, there's nothing I can do. I will continue to visit her and hope that one day she'll get better. But I don't know if that will happen."

Gabe pulled her close as they walked in silence for a few moments.

Rory smiled unexpectedly. "But I'm happy. Especially now that Ned has come to work here on the Island. He's enjoying working poolside and at the watercraft rental space. He's happier now and is grateful to be here. I feel like I'm starting to get to know my half brother. The real Ned is a lot like my Dad. Playful and always teasing. I'm thankful he lives near us now."

"I'm glad. Family is important. It's been a blessing to have your aunts living so close to us. They love helping out with our little girl." Gabe chuckled. "And it's comical to watch them fight over who will get to hold her."

Rory giggled. "I love my aunts. I always imagined that my mom would've been like one of them if she would have been alive to see me grow up, marry and have children."

"I'm sure she would have been the best mom." Gabe stopped her suddenly and pulled her into his arms. "Just like you are the best wife and mom anywhere."

"Aww Gabe. You make me feel wonderful and so loved." Rory slipped her arms around his neck. He tugged her closer.

Gabe leaned down and kissed her forehead and then her nose. "That's because you are wonderful, special and very loved."

His wife's violet eyes filled with tears and stared deep into his soul.

"Rory my love, you have stolen my heart. It's your courage, determination and compassion that tugged on my heart strings since the first day I saw you. That scared little girl — who asked if I would promise to marry her when we got older — won my heart from the first day.

"Only now you are no longer a scared little girl, but a grown woman who is brave, beautiful and kind. And now you have an even bigger heart."

Gabe expelled a shaky breath. "We've shared many memories through the years some good, some not so good. I'm sad to say, fear held me back from being vulnerable and allowing myself to accept your love."

He swallowed in an effort to hold back tears that clogged his throat. "You might think I saved you but it's really the other way around. Your acceptance and love saved me and I was able to see for the first time who I really am and the treasure that you are. I love you, Rory."

No longer was their marriage fake. They now had a real marriage based on love and commitment.

With his arms around her waist he lowered his head and gently placed his lips on hers.

The sweetness of Rory's kiss intoxicated him. He breathed deeply of her floral scent loving the way her arms held tightly to him.

Having Rory in his arms, felt like he was accepted simply for who he was.

Having Rory in his arms, felt like coming home.

RORY'S HEART pounded hard and slow as his lips claimed hers.

Her knees weakened as her husband took control of the kiss.

Gabe kissed her in the way she'd always dreamed he would with a sense of strength behind every movement of his lips on hers.

It wasn't the passion of his kiss that made Rory catch her breath. It was the gentle intimacy as he held her close to his heart in his strong, gentle arms.

She tightened her arms around his neck urging herself closer to her husband returning his kiss with all the fire she had inside.

His love had melted her heart and turned her emotions into a hot messy puddle of bliss.

She loved every minute.

Rory felt like she'd waited forever for Gabe to love her giving up hope that it would actually happen for them.

Believing that she wasn't good enough to be loved by someone like Gabe Stevenson had all been lies.

Maddie Winslow had tried to convince her that she wasn't worthy to be Gabe's wife and that he would regret marrying her.

Those had all been lies inflicted on Rory because Maddie was jealous.

She saw that clearly now.

Gabe really did love her.

He didn't feel sorry for her.

He had setup security around the Island to keep her safe and helped her expand her skin care products because he loved her. He'd risked his life to save her from Aunt Mal's cruelty, all because he loved her.

Now Gabe and his family had become her own.

Rory truly belonged to a bigger family again. For such a long time she'd felt lonely and abandoned since her parents died and she believed things would never change.

Becoming Gabe's wife had changed everything for her. It was the best feeling in the world.

Her heart overflowed with gratitude.

Gabe ended the kiss his blue eyes glowing with tenderness.

"I have a surprise for you."

"What is it?"

"Since the fire we only hired people to clean up and board up that side of the house. But I thought since our family is growing we could hire a restorative team to expand and restore Grand's old Hunting Lodge."

Rory smiled. "I would love that. What a wonderful surprise."

"Well we do need to get that house fixed up like new so we can have more children." Her husband chuckled his eyes crinkling with playfulness.

"That would be wonderful." Her eyes glimmered brightly with love and she reached up to kiss his cheek.

"You've taught me how important it is to embrace the love of family." He kissed her forehead and they turned together to watch the sunlight glistening on the water.

"Near this tree by this little bay is the same spot I saw you one year ago." Rory grinned as she remembered. "I was a wet, soggy mess and a little rude to you."

"We both needed to grow beyond our mistaken beliefs and fears." Gabe tilted her chin up and with gentle fingers looked deep into her eyes. "When I made that marriage promise years ago it was the best decision I ever made because it brought me to you."

He kissed her lips tenderly. "I love you so much Rory."

At his words a lone tear escaped and slid down her cheek.

She knew she would never get tired of hearing her husband say those words.

"I love you too."

EPILOGUE

uke

A TODDLER'S deep belly laugh and a baby's soft giggle was carried along with the wind in the wide open sandy beach where the Stevenson family gathered.

Luke Stevenson grinned as he watched his brother Adam tickle his son Daniel. Nearby Adam's wife Elle held their new baby girl who squealed with delight as her mommy planted raspberry kisses on her belly.

His brother Zach, his mom and grandparents played with the three other grandchildren while Jack and Bella enjoyed a quiet chat with Gabe and Rory.

Restless, Luke stood to his feet and walked along the beach thinking about his life.

The peaceful atmosphere here on Walker's Island was a great place for that.

Reaching down he picked up a smooth flat stone and flicked his wrist sending it skipping across the water.

As he watched the rock follow a straight line, he questioned his own life. Why didn't his life follow a straight path? Why were there so many curveballs tossed his way?

Hearing more laughter, a numbness blanketed him all the way down to his toes. He wanted more spontaneous laughter and joy in his life.

Seeing his brothers loving life with their wives caused a churning in his belly. He was happy for them but envied their happiness at the same time.

His brow furrowed as he remembered the woman that slipped through his fingers years ago.

"Hey man." Gabe leaned over and bumped his shoulder.

Startled out of his musings, Luke turned to his brother a half-smile lighting up his otherwise serious face.

"Hey, Gabe. You've outdone yourself. This place looks incredible. With all the setbacks you've had, you deserve to have time to play and enjoy the beauty around you. Grand would be proud of all you've accomplished on the Island." Luke looked up to the large green space where the newly renovated Hunting Lodge sat proudly in the sunlight.

Gabe turned his head and followed his gaze. "Looking at Grand's old place now, it's hard to believe we had a devastating fire." Gabe paused for a moment and sighed. "It's nice to have the renovations finished. And I think you're right. Grand would be pleased that we've been able to renovate and still keep much of the original place intact."

Luke nodded admiring the view. "You've done well Gabe. I'm happy you got what you wanted, including the woman you love."

Gabe reached down to pick up a flat stone, skipping it across the water. "Thanks Luke. It feels good." His brother gave him a sideways glance his forehead puckered with concern. "There's a woman out there just waiting for you, Luke."

"I don't think so. It's too late for me. I already had my chance, remember?" Luke shook his head silently and scuffed his sandalled feet against a few loose stones.

Gabe's chuckle was one of undisguised disbelief.

His brother thumped a hand on his shoulder, forcing Luke to look at him. "Luke, you can't let what happened seven years ago sentence you to a life of loneliness."

Luke shrugged, unsure of what to say. Trust Gabe to hit a little too close to home when it came to understanding his fears.

Reluctantly, Luke's gaze met his brother's probing blue eyes. "You can have what you want. It's not too late. Just because Audra chose to run away on your wedding day, doesn't mean you're destined to live life alone."

"Maybe I am. I mean, who's to say that won't happen again?" Luke swallowed back the fear that threatened to choke him. "There was no rhyme or reason for Audra to leave me at the altar."

Gabe hesitated before adding softly. "Until she wrote that letter of apology."

"Yeah, at least it was helpful to know that my fiance discovered she loved somebody else before she became my wife. That's something, I guess." Luke sighed heavily.

Luke stepped away from his brother and reached for another stone. His thoughts went back to the woman who left him at the altar.

Ever since that day years ago, Luke had questioned whether there would be any woman again to whom he'd be willing to commit to. He had analyzed and tried to figure out what went wrong years ago. Why didn't he notice the signs that he was losing his fiance?

With an angry flick of his wrist he sent the smooth stone sailing across the water. It was the greatest distance he'd thrown yet.

His brother kicked at a few stones and Luke turned to look his way.

Gabe spoke softly. "I know it's tough to trust again when you've already been burned by love. I've been through that myself."

Luke remembered how Gabe's old girlfriend Maddie had manipulated him. Reluctantly he nodded, admitting his brother also had his share of hurt. "Sorry, man."

"It's okay. I just want you to know you're not alone." Gabe paused before continuing. "Your birthday is coming up soon and with it the deadline to receive your inheritance."

"I know." Luke had done nothing but think about Grand's ridiculous will requirement these past few months.

"So, do you want that land with all those mineral rights that Grand left you in his will?"

Luke was quiet for a moment, looking skyward before he faced his brother. He knew Gabe would continue to ask questions until he got answers. He might as well clear

the air now. "I do want that land. There's just one problem. To my way of thinking the price is a little too high."

"You just haven't found the right woman, Luke." Gabe
sent him a lopsided grin.

"I don't think falling in love is for me, man." Luke
shook his head certain as he could be of this truth.
"Besides, I'm not even dating anyone right now. Haven't
dated a woman seriously for years."

Gabe grinned. "I think you'll be surprised at how you
will simply find the right woman when it's your turn for
love, Luke." The corner of his lips turned up into a
knowing smile.

Luke shook his head, disbelief oozing it's way through
every pore in his body.

His life-of-the-party brother might have found love,
but it was too difficult for a man like him who was
reserved and held his feelings close to his chest.

Besides, he needed someone who wasn't afraid of
adventure and who could appreciate his maverick ways.

He needed someone who would treasure family and
building a home together.

He needed someone who would stay by his side and
not run far away from him the first chance she got.

Where would he possibly find this jewel of a woman?

No, Luke couldn't see himself finding a woman who
had all those wonderful qualities anytime soon.

Maybe this time he would have to accept, that finding
real love simply wasn't possible for a man like him.

MELODY ARCHER

READY FOR THE NEXT BOOK IN THIS SERIES? START READING LUKE'S STORY: "THE BILLIONAIRE'S MARRIAGE BARTER!"

Luke Stevenson is a maverick who longs to own the large piece of mineral-rich earth left to him by his late Great Grandfather.

There's just one obstacle standing in his way: **According to Grand's will, Luke must find a woman to marry by his 27th birthday in order to receive his inheritance.**

He only has 5 weeks until the deadline.

Razelle has grown up as an only child hidden away from the world by a strict and selfish Mother. Reeling from a painful childhood, Raz longs for freedom. Desperate to find escape, at night Raz helps bring healing to those living nearby at a camp for the homeless.

When she discovers Luke with a leg wound, Raz devotes a lot of her time to help him heal. After her Mother learns what happened, in anger Raz's Mother places tougher restrictions on her. Now, not only is her freedom in jeopardy but so is her heart.

Luke comes up with a plan to protect her with a marriage-in-name-only. Razelle agrees.
Will being forced together steer them towards love or pull them farther apart?

ALSO BY MELODY ARCHER

Clean Billionaire Fake Marriage Romance Series

Book 1: The Billionaire's Marriage Bargain

Book 2: The Billionaire's Marriage Contract

Book 3: The Billionaire's Marriage Promise

Book 4: The Billionaire's Marriage Barter

Book 5: The Billionaire's Marriage Pledge

7 Brides for 7 Cowboys, Small Town Sweet Western Romance Series

Book 1: The Forgiven Cowboy's Best Friend

Book 2: The Redeemed Cowboy's Secret Baby

Book 3: The Honorable Cowboy's Convenient Marriage

Book 4: The Wounded Cowboy's Beauty Bride

Books 5, 6 & 7 still to come…

Grab the next book in your favorite series when you visit my Author Website below:

www.memorablefictionbooks.com

ABOUT THE AUTHOR

Melody Archer lives in Alberta with her husband and their four young adults.

Recently, her oldest son married and their family has been enjoying getting to know their oldest son's new wife from Brazil ~ their new daughter-in-love. :)

She loves new and classic romantic movies, green smoothies and going on adventures with her family.

Melody would love to connect with you :)

ACKNOWLEDGMENTS

Thank you to all the wonderful people who helped me with this book.

To my cover designer, Wilette from Red Leaf Book Design, thank you for designing this gorgeous book cover.

Thank you also, to my proofreader Cathy who patiently read through each chapter, helping me make this story so much better.

A big thanks to all my wonderful Advanced Readers (my ARC reading team), who faithfully read and left reviews of this book.

Lastly, a huge thanks to three of my young adult children who read through the manuscript, giving me all kinds of great suggestions on how to make this a better story.
Thank you everyone. I really appreciate you!:)